"Those haughty airs don't go with all the leg you're showing," the stranger observed.

"What are you doing?" Callie demanded as he reached up and grabbed the first branch with no trouble.

"I'm coming to rescue you, of course. I read all the King Arthur legends and always wanted to rescue a maiden in distress."

Callie's breath caught in her lungs as his hard hands encircled her waist and turned her around. Her small, cold nose was pressed up against his shirt and the odor of fresh linen, soap, and the more elusive, slightly musky aroma of his skin filled her nostrils. Her breasts tingled where they were pressed against his chest, and her lower body shivered with reaction to the feel of his hard-muscled thighs pressing into her soft flesh.

Skillfully, he started the downward climb, then Callie was swung gently to the ground.

"Thank you very much for your assistance, sir." Callie gave the tall stranger a dismissing nod of her head, but unfortunately he didn't move.

"You mean I don't get to keep you?"

Dear Reader:

As the months go by, we continue to receive word from you that SECOND CHANCE AT LOVE romances are providing you with the kind of romantic entertainment you're looking for. In your letters you've voiced enthusiastic support for SECOND CHANCE AT LOVE, you've shared your thoughts on how personally meaningful the books are, and you've suggested ideas and changes for future books. Although we can't always reply to your letters as quickly as we'd like, please be assured that we appreciate your comments. Your thoughts are all-important to us!

We're glad many of you have come to associate SECOND CHANCE AT LOVE books with our butterfly trademark. We think the butterfly is a perfect symbol of the reaffirmation of life and thrilling new love that SECOND CHANCE AT LOVE heroines and heroes find together in each story. We hope you keep asking for the "butterfly books," and that, when you buy one—whether by a favorite author or a talented new writer—you're sure of a good read. You can trust all SECOND CHANCE AT LOVE books to live up to the high standards of romantic fiction you've come to expect.

So happy reading, and keep your letters coming!

With warm wishes,

Ellen Edwards

Ellen Edwards
SECOND CHANCE AT LOVE
The Berkley/Jove Publishing Group
200 Madison Avenue
New York, NY 10016

Second Chance at Love
REGENCY

THE EARL'S FANCY
CHARLOTTE HINES

A
SECOND CHANCE AT LOVE
BOOK

THE EARL'S FANCY

First edition published December 1982

First printing

"Second Chance at Love" and the butterfly emblem are trademarks belonging to Jove Publications, Inc.

Printed in the United States of America

Second Chance at Love books are published by
The Berkley/Jove Publishing Group
200 Madison Avenue, New York, NY 10016

THE EARL'S FANCY

- 1 -

"WILL HE LIVE, Dr. Adams?" The slender woman whispered the question as soon as the doctor appeared in the doorway of the master bedroom.

He closed the door behind him quietly and looked down into worried brown eyes, red-rimmed with fatigue and weeping.

"Sir Jason's a very sick man, Miss Callie," he answered, sidestepping the question, "but he's resting comfortably right now. Do sit down for a minute and we'll discuss his condition."

Dr. Adams guided her to a mahogany stool under the tall, narrow window in the broad hallway and gently pushed her onto it.

"I'm not a child, Doctor." Callie braced herself visibly. "Don't dither. Tell me the truth."

"No, you're five-and-twenty now, aren't you? And it seems like just yesterday that you were born." Dr. Adams shook his head and then recalled himself to the unpleasant task at hand. "Sir Jason isn't any worse, Miss Callie, but

1

he's still a very sick man. This seizure was quite severe, and your father is seventy years old."

"But he won't die?" Callie demanded.

"I don't know," the doctor replied bluntly. "Usually if a seizure is going to kill, it does so at once. The fact that your father has survived the first day without losing any ground can be taken as a hopeful sign. With a great deal of luck and careful nursing, he may recover."

Callie's eyes shone with tears. "Oh, thank you. Thank you so much." Her voice caught on a sob and she gulped it back before she continued. "He'll have careful nursing. You need have no fear of that."

"I don't doubt it for a minute." The doctor chuckled dryly. "I'm well acquainted with Nanny Weeks. No one would dare not recover with her in charge; she'd take it as a personal affront."

"Which brings us to another point, Miss Callie," the doctor continued. "I can't stress enough how important it is that Sir Jason not be worried about anything. Worry is liable to bring on another seizure, and another one would undoubtedly kill him."

"I won't forget, Doctor," Callie replied evenly, "but there shouldn't be anything to worry him. I've been running the estate myself for the past seven years. Ever since the old bailiff died. Papa was always more interested in his study of Shakespeare than whether the fields should be planted in wheat or pease."

"Yes, I know," the doctor acknowledged, keeping to himself the opinion that Sir Jason Sutcliff had been more than a little selfish in dumping the worries of his small, unprofitable estate on the slender shoulders of his eldest daughter while he continued to live in a literary dream world of his own. Callie would have denounced the thought angrily, despite its truth. She, as well as her three sisters, was devoted to her vague, forgetful father and would never hear a word against him.

"He is worried though, Miss Callie, and not about the estate, but about you four girls. I think for the first time he realizes that he's not immortal, and he's concerned about what will happen to you when he's gone."

"Well he needn't be." Callie raised her chin. "We'll manage."

"I'm sure you will," the doctor replied, though privately he had doubts. "But you must convince your father of that fact. For all his vague habits, Sir Jason really is a very shrewd man. You'll need to have some kind of plan to present to him. Something that will put his mind to rest." Dr. Adams broke off as the elderly butler shuffled down the hall toward him.

"Yes, Price?" Callie smiled affectionately at the stooped little man.

"You have a visitor, Miss Callie."

"A visitor! But I'm not receiving visitors now."

"I told Mrs. Sutcliff that, Miss Callie, but she just pushed past me. She said that she wanted to talk to you." Price's faded blue eyes looked worried. "I'm sorry, but . . ."

"That's all right, Price. I'll be down in a minute," Callie reassured him, knowing full well that the frail butler wouldn't have stood a chance against her cousin-by-marriage. Once Joan Sutcliff made up her mind to do something, nothing would sway her from her course. Little matters like good manners or consideration for others would never enter her thinking.

Callie stood up and shook out her long blue skirts. "May I see you out, Doctor?"

"Yes. Sir Jason will be fine for now, but don't hesitate to send for me if the situation should change. Not that I expect it to," he hurried on as he saw her frown. "You and Nanny Weeks should be able to cope. I left her complete instructions."

"Thank you, Dr. Adams. I appreciate your kindness," Callie murmured as they walked down the long, chill hallway that was already darkening in the fading light of the short January day.

"Goodbye, Dr. Adams. Godspeed." Callie stood on the red brick steps in front of the graceful Queen Anne house as the doctor heaved his bulk up into his ancient landaulet. Idly, she watched him click the reins to prod the equally ancient horse, postponing the moment when she had to face Joan Sutcliff. An icy blast of wind hit her with devastating force, and, with a final wave at the doctor's retreating figure, she went inside.

Price was waiting for her in the foyer as Callie closed the heavy oak door softly behind her.

"I suppose I'd best see our visitor and get it over with." Callie grimaced. "Where did you put her, Price? In the morning room?"

"I didn't put her anywhere, Miss Callie. She just went."

"And where did she 'just went'?"

"The main salon. If you should want me, I'll be in the kitchen. When that wind comes off the sea, it's the warmest room in the house. Will you be wanting tea served to Mrs. Sutcliff?"

"I think not," Callie replied frowning. "Anyone insensitive enough to force herself into a house of sickness can hardly expect to be treated to refreshments and polite social conversation. I'll find out why she came and then get rid of her. It shouldn't take me long. Please ask my sisters to meet me in the morning room as soon as possible."

"Of course, Miss Callie. They'll want to know what the doctor said about Sir Jason."

Callie watched him shuffle toward the back of the house before she turned toward the main salon. She found Joan Sutcliff fingering the worn blue damask drapes which outlined the three eight-foot-high windows facing the rolling south lawn.

"Contemplating changes, Joan?" Callie took exception to the woman's proprietary manner. "You aren't mistress here yet."

"It's only a matter of time before my Gilmer inherits the estate," Joan said complacently, turning toward Callie. "In all practicality, you cannot expect Sir Jason to survive this seizure."

"We aren't discussing practicalities, we're discussing my father, whom I happen to love very much!"

"Love is a vastly overrated emotion." Joan's dispassionate voice flicked Callie's already raw nerves. "Besides, your love can hardly make any difference to your father's health."

Callie swallowed the angry protest she wanted to make to Joan's insensitive words. That Joan meant exactly what she'd said, Callie had not the slightest doubt. Long ago she'd learned that Joan had not an ounce of sentiment in her. The daughter of a very successful merchant, Joan had married Callie's cousin Gilmer, trading her rich dowry for entrance into the aristocracy. Love had had nothing to do with the bargain she struck, and neither had respect. Joan ruled the weak Gilmer with an iron rod.

"Why are you here, Joan?" Callie asked bluntly. "I'm much too busy to bandy words with you."

"Gilmer and I will be going up to London tomorrow to open our town house for the season, and I want to settle some details before we go," Joan replied calmly.

"Details?" Callie echoed, her tired mind not grasping Joan's meaning.

"Of the transfer of the estate to Gilmer. Sir Jason can't possibly linger for more than a few weeks, and it would be very inconvenient for us to come all the way back here just to handle some points which can easily be cleared up before we leave. Now, then," Joan continued, totally ignoring Callie's outraged gasp, "you, Olivia, and Diana are certainly capable of finding suitable positions in genteel households after the funeral. However, I should hope that no one would have to tell me my duty as regards the cripple." Joan gave Callie a sanctimonious smile.

"Her name is Rosalind!" Callie snapped.

"Whatever," Joan said dismissingly. "I wouldn't want it said that I'd turned her out. You may tell her that, provided she's willing to make herself useful, she may stay as a companion to my daughter."

"Your generosity astounds me!" Callie's sarcasm was biting, but Joan took the words at face value.

"I should hope I know my duties as a lady toward the less fortunate." Joan's complacent words lit the fuse of Callie's temper.

"Lady!" Callie's scornful eyes swept over Joan's bulky proportions. "That's something you'll never be, Joan Sutcliff. Coming here on such a tasteless errand! I have no intention of discussing anything with you. When the time comes," Callie's voice faltered, but she steadied it and went on, "our lawyer will discuss the transfer of The Meadings with Gilmer. The Meadings is his inheritance, not yours."

"If you're hoping to gammon Gilmer into allowing you to remain here after Sir Jason's death, put the idea out of your head." Joan pulled on a pair of pale pink kid gloves. "Gilmer will do exactly as he's told. Since you're going to be so unreasonable, I'll go. I doubt that we shall have cause ever to see each other again. Goodbye." Joan gave Callie an angry nod and sailed out of the room.

Callie sighed wearily, silently acknowledging the stupidity of what she'd just done. Angering her cousin's wife could serve no useful purpose and would only make a bad situation worse. But how much worse could it get? she asked herself. Callie didn't have the slightest doubt that Joan meant every word she had said. The minute Gilmer inherited the estate, they would all be homeless, unless Joan let Rosalind stay because it would make her feel like Lady Bountiful to dispense charity to her husband's crippled cousin. Not that Rosalind was really crippled, Callie mentally denied Joan's allegation. Aside from a slight limp, only her right arm had been affected by the withering fever she'd contracted five years ago. Rosalind wasn't going to be left to Joan's tender mercies, no matter what.

Callie rubbed her forehead in frustration. This situation would never have arisen if only things had worked out differently seven years ago. She would now be a young matron instead of a spinster, and there would have been no question of her sisters' future. They would have lived with her until she could have arranged suitable marriages for them. If only! Callie grimaced as the bitter memories flooded her mind.

Seven years ago this coming spring, her cousin Frederick had arrived at The Meadings to honor the betrothal contract which their father had arranged eight years before. A tall, slightly built young man with curly brown hair which was continually tumbling down over his dreamy blue eyes, Frederick was the living embodiment of all Callie's romantic fantasies. From his exquisitely tailored clothes to his propensity for writing poetry, he was Callie's masculine ideal, and she had tumbled head-over-heels in love with him. A love she had made no attempt to hide.

Her happiness had reached its zenith a few weeks before the wedding when Frederick had taken her for a walk in the gardens and whispered words of love to her. Callie still remembered the rapture of his lips against hers as he'd pressed hot kisses on her trembling mouth.

As the days went by and the wedding drew closer, Frederick began to spend less and less time at The Meadings, but Callie, moving in a daze of happiness, hadn't questioned him, accepting as natural that a small country estate would be very boring to a man used to the amusements of London. Exactly what he could be doing to entertain himself in the equally small village of Thornton Dene never entered her mind. It was enough that he was near her. Callie was deep in her dreams of their perfect married life, dreams fueled by the increasing fervor of his kisses.

It came as a complete shock when, only days before the wedding, Frederick told her that, despite their longstanding betrothal, he couldn't force himself to go through with the wedding. Moreover, he was going to marry a beautiful daughter of a wealthy grain merchant who lived nearby.

In an effort to defend himself from the dazed incredulity in Callie's face, he had laid the blame for his defection on her, citing her lack of looks and dowry and her managing ways. She had nothing to attract a man, he'd insisted, apparently conveniently forgetting the impassioned kisses he'd shared with her.

Love, Callie had thought with bitter self-mockery, love was for women who possessed beauty and wealth. Love wasn't for a plain, thin slip of a girl with nothing to offer but her heart.

Callie had handed him back his ring silently, and walked away, unable to listen to his excuses any longer. Moving in a fog of misery, she had canceled the wedding arrangements and buried her dreams of love and marriage deep in her heart, knowing now that she had neither the looks nor the money to bring them to fruition.

"Are you alone, Callie?" a soft voice called from the doorway.

Jerking her mind back to the present, Callie looked up to see Rosalind peeping in. She smiled at the shy girl.

"Yes, I'm afraid I wounded dear Joan's sensibilities and she departed in high dudgeon."

"What did she want? She never comes to call."

"Oh," Callie replied vaguely, "she's heard about Papa and came to ask after him. If you'll get Olivia and Diana, I'll tell you what Dr. Adams said."

"Yes, please, just a minute." Rosalind hurried out, her one foot dragging a little in her haste.

The two older sisters must have been waiting in the hall because all three were back almost immediately.

"Rosalind said that the doctor has told you about Papa?" Olivia, Callie's junior by four years, asked the question that was in all their minds.

"Yes, and don't look so worried. Dr. Adams thinks that with careful nursing Papa will recover."

"Thank God!" Diana, just eighteen and highly sensitive, burst into tears.

"Don't cry, love," Callie automatically bolstered her. "You'll make your eyes red. Besides, there's more to it than that."

"How much more?" Olivia nibbled her lower lip worriedly.

"Rosalind, please help—" Callie began.

"No," Rosalind refused flatly. "Please, Callie, don't send me away. I have a right to know, too. Just because my arm is useless doesn't mean that I am."

"It isn't that at all, Rosalind," Callie responded quickly. "It's just that I've always thought of you as the baby of the family and it's hard to change. But you're right. This is going to affect you as much as it is Olivia, Diana, and me. You have a right to help us decide what to do." She glanced at each sister in turn. "Dr. Adams says that Papa is worried about what's to become of us after he dies, and that it's very bad for him. He must be kept free from all worry."

"That's strange," Olivia said. "He's never worried about it before."

"It probably never occurred to him before." Callie smiled indulgently. "He's been too immersed in that book on Shakespeare he's writing to notice that we've grown up."

"I wish that Mama were still alive." Olivia stood and wandered over to the fireplace, where she began carefully tracing the anthemion carvings on the Adam mantel. "She always had such good ideas."

"Yes," Callie agreed with a sigh, "she did, didn't she. But feeling sorry for ourselves isn't going to help a bit. For Papa's sake as well as our own, we've got to come up with some plans for the future."

"Can't we just stay here?" Rosalind asked. "We could share one of those big rooms facing the west lawn. That would still leave six bedrooms for Joan and Gilmer."

Callie hesitated briefly and then decided on total candor. "Joan has always said that you could stay, Rosalind, if you make yourself useful, but that the rest of us must go."

"I imagine she means to turn me into a personal servant for that horrible little daughter of hers. Then she can brag about how she gave her crippled cousin a home," Rosalind stated with unchildlike perception.

"Rosalind!" Callie protested.

"It's true," Rosalind insisted. "If you don't mind, Callie, I'd rather stay with you."

"Of course we'll all stay together," Callie assured her, "but the pressing problem is how. How can we possibly earn enough money to live on?"

"You're a good estate manager, Callie," Diana said. "Couldn't you get a place? Those positions usually have houses with them."

"I could, except for two things," Callie replied. "First, my farm knowledge is limited to small Kentish farms on the sea; and, secondly, no one is going to hire a woman when there are scores of men to be had."

"Are there scores?" Olivia asked.

"Unfortunately, yes." Callie sighed. "And the longer this

war with Napoleon lasts, the worse it gets. I could go down to Brighton tomorrow and hire thirty men who know more about farming than I do."

"Well, then, what about one of us being a governess?" Diana suggested.

"We haven't the refinements," Olivia vetoed the idea. "None of us play the piano, speak Italian or French, paint in watercolors..."

"It isn't necessary to be so depressingly accurate!" Diana broke in.

"And besides, governesses never have dependents," Olivia finished.

"Why don't we write a book?" Rosalind cried, bouncing up and down on the sofa in excitement at the idea. "We've read hundreds of books, and Papa would be so pleased."

"Only if we wrote a scholarly work, and since the only thing we read are novels..." Callie allowed her voice to trail away.

"Besides," Olivia added, "none of us can spell, and I don't think you can make enough to live on just writing novels."

"But then what can we do to earn enough to live on?" Rosalind demanded.

Silence greeted her pertinent question until finally Callie said, "As far as I can see, the only hope we have is for one of us to marry and the rest to live with her."

"Marriage!" Rosalind sounded horrified.

"You are right." Diana considered Callie's words. "There really isn't very much a gentlewoman can do to acquire money, except marry. Olivia—" Diana turned to her sister—"you and Emmet Hadley were as thick as inkle-weavers before he lost an arm at Badajos last fall. I know he's been home from Spain only a week, but is there any chance..."

"No!" Olivia shouted and then blushed hotly as the other three looked dumbfounded at her vehemence. "It wasn't, it isn't. He fell in love with a Spanish lady and is only waiting for the war to be over before he sends for her to join him here in England," Olivia stated baldly. "He told me when

I went to visit him the day he arrived home."

"Oh, Livy," Diana sympathized. "I'm so sorry."

"It's all right," Olivia claimed. "I don't mind a fig. It just means that I can't marry him, and there isn't anyone else in the neighborhood except the vicar, and if it comes to a choice between starving and the Reverend Marston, I think I'd rather starve."

"There'll be some guests at Squire Varden's soon," Rosalind said.

"What guests?" Callie asked, her interest piqued.

"The squire's younger brother, Tristam, is bringing down some swells from London to visit," Rosalind explained, "and Kitty says that one of them is the Earl of Rutledge."

"Kitty?" Olivia frowned.

"Our kitchen maid's sister. She works at the Hall. The squire just got his brother's letter yesterday. Why don't we just take this earl? An earl should have lots of money."

"Not all earls have money, Rosalind. Some are almost as purse-pinched as we are."

"Not this one," Rosalind insisted. "Kitty says he's swimming in lard."

"Kitty seems to be a fount of wisdom." Olivia laughed. "But even if she is right, how would we go about capturing him? Just invite him to tea and tell him we're hanging out for a rich husband and does he fancy any of us?"

"Ada would help." Callie recalled the squire's wife with affection. "She would think it terribly romantic."

"*Isabella's Quest*," Diana inserted parenthetically.

"What?" Callie stared blankly at her sister.

"*Isabella's Quest*. You remember," Diana continued excitedly. "It was that book about the daughter of a duke who went to London to find a rich husband to save her father's estates. It tells exactly how she found one, too."

"I remember." Callie caught her meaning. "We could use the book as an outline. We'll have to adapt it because this isn't London, but the basic strategy should be the same," she elaborated on Diana's idea.

Callie did not seriously believe that they had any hope of inveigling this unknown earl into marriage, but at least the attempt would help to keep her sisters's minds off the frailty of their father's health and the precariousness of their own position.

Besides, Callie told herself as the idea began to grow, it wasn't beyond the realm of possibility. Wealthy men had been known to fall madly in love with beautiful young women before, and, while it certainly didn't happen with the ease and frequency that it did in novels, it did happen. Callie remembered the penniless Gunning sisters who had taken London society by storm fifty years earlier. Why, one of them had married two dukes, and all they wanted had been one earl. If correctly handled, there was a very slim chance she and her sisters might be able to do it. Callie's thoughts hardened into resolve. What had been done before could be done again. For the sake of her sisters, she had to try. She had no alternative, she admitted bleakly.

"Who's going to marry him?" Rosalind asked. "I'm only fourteen, so it can't be me."

"Well." Callie looked at her to middle sisters, comparing Olivia's blond prettiness with Diana's golden loveliness. "If you wouldn't mind so terribly, Diana, it really ought to be you because you're the prettiest. And, if you haven't a dowry, the next best thing to have is beauty. One look at you and he'll be bowled over."

"But what about you, Callie?" Rosalind protested. "You'd make a lovely countess. You always have such great ideas."

"Men don't marry women for their ideas. They marry them for their dowries or for what they look like, and mouse-brown hair, brown eyes, and a skinny figure don't look like much." Callie's tone was caustic from bitter experience. "Now," she briskly changed the subject, "are you willing to marry this earl, Diana?"

"Of course I'll marry him, and then we can all live together at his family seat while he spends his time in London," Diana predicted blithely, her knowledge of the *haut ton* and their marital habits gleaned from the *Gazette* and Ada Varden's gossip. If Callie, with her greater common sense, felt that Diana's view was overly optimistic, she kept the opinion strictly to herself. Diana, for all her beauty, was a gentle girl of exquisite sensibilities who needed a great deal of encouraging and bolstering to meet the daily demands of life. Hopefully, this unknown earl would be a kind man willing to cherish her.

"We're agreed then?" Callie looked at her three sisters. "We're going to capture this earl for Diana?"

Three heads nodded happily back at her.

"I'll find *Isabella's Quest*," Rosalind volunteered. "I think Nanny has it up in her room."

"The hypocrite!" Callie laughed. "After all her complaints about how purple prose would lead us all to perdition, and then to find her reading the 'filth' t'ings'." Callie mimicked Nanny's broad Yorkshire dialect that thirty-five years on the Kentish coast hadn't altered.

"Maybe Nanny thinks she's too old to be led astray," Rosalind suggested.

"Be that as it may, it would be best if we didn't tell her about our plan," Callie said. "She'd be bound to object and, to be honest, if it doesn't work, I don't know what we'll do."

"You'll think of something, Callie," Rosalind assured her with all the resiliency of youth. "You always do."

The fact that there was quite a bit of difference between managing a small estate and arranging the marriage of a penniless girl to a wealthy peer, Callie refrained from mentioning. There was no purpose to be served by destroying Rosalind's confidence. Let her keep her dreams as long as possible. There would be plenty of time for her to face up to the hard facts of life if they couldn't bring the earl up to scratch.

"Miss Callie."

Callie looked up at Price, who stood in the doorway.

"Nanny says would you come and see your Papa? He's asking for you, and she doesn't want to refuse him in case it upsets him."

"Of course, I'm coming immediately." Callie jumped up and hurried out. She swiftly climbed the graceful oak staircase, her feet flying over the faded green carpet as her mind feverishly sorted through the reasons why her father might wish to see her.

"Well, missy, you took your time." Nanny sniffed from beside the head of Sir Jason's bed, her scolding reassuringly normal. A tiny woman who barely reached five feet, she wore her sparse gray hair screwed back into a tight bun. Her lined, wrinkled face was faintly reminiscent of a shriveled apple, but her beady black eyes were alert and shrewd, although at the moment they were rimmed with fatigue.

"What's wrong?" Callie whispered, not sure whether her father was asleep or not.

"Nothing, my dear," Sir Jason answered, his voice a thin thread of sound. "I just wanted to talk to you."

"That would be lovely," Callie said, keeping her voice purposefully cheerful. "I have a few things to say to you, too. Just a minute, Papa," Callie said as he started to speak. "I have a message for Nanny. You close your eyes and rest. I'll be right back." Motioning for Nanny to follow her, Callie retreated across the large room to the door.

"I'll sit with him for a while, Nanny. You must take a nap."

"A nap!" Nanny sounded outraged. "What would I be needing a nap for, missy?"

"You haven't been to bed since yesterday afternoon. Please, Nanny." Callie put an arm around the ruffled little woman. "We'll need you later, and if you don't rest now, you'll be too tired to help."

"That's true," Nanny agreed, weakening.

"And if you're too tired, you might fall asleep just when Papa needed you," Callie concluded with satisfaction.

"Very well, missy, but try not to let him talk too much. It tires him."

"Do you know what he wanted me for?"

"He keeps saying something about Master Gilmer looking after you girls when he dies." Nanny frowned. "But he must remember Mrs. Sutcliff. She wouldn't lift a hand to help you."

"It doesn't matter, Nanny." Callie tried to make her voice

sound bright. "We've decided that marriage will solve all our problems."

To her surprise, Nanny accepted her words at face value. "That'd be Master Emmet and Miss Olivia. Everyone knew they were going to get riveted when he got back from that dreadful war. When's the wedding to be?"

"Well . . ." Callie briefly debated telling Nanny the truth before deciding against it. Nanny was every bit as much a worrier as Papa was. "Emmet still hasn't recovered from losing that arm, and then, with Papa so sick, they decided a formal announcement wouldn't be at all the thing. Right now it's still a secret. Perhaps they'll be married quietly in the spring."

"Good." Nanny nodded her head. "Your Papa couldn't stand the excitement of a big do. Besides, a quiet wedding will be cheaper," she added practically, "and while we've been getting along, there certainly isn't any money to spare. Now, you go sit with Sir Jason and I'll take a nap. But only a short one, hear?"

"Yes, Nanny, I hear." She opened the door and Nanny slipped through. Softly, Callie closed it behind her, then leaned against the door, allowing the peace and tranquillity of the room to steal over her.

She quietly made her way over to the huge canopied bed and sat down on the straight-backed chair beside it, intently studying her father's still form. His slight body was barely visible under the plump comforter, and Callie swallowed as the full import of his frailty hit her. Always a small, thin man, he seemed to have shrunk visibly in the past two days. His normal rosy complexion was now gray, faintly tinged with blue, and even his wispy, white hair seemed to have a grayish cast to it this evening.

As Callie watched, his eyelids fluttered up, and his pale blue eyes lit with pleasure at seeing her there.

"Calpurnia, my dear," he murmured. "My dear Calpurnia."

"Calpurnia?" Callie laughed, trying not to burst into tears at the love in his voice. "You haven't called me Calpurnia since I was twelve and convinced Olivia that she could fly off the stable roof. Poor thing, she was lucky all she broke was her arm."

"Olivia's such a sweet child, but she has no gumption. She needs someone to look after her. She needs..." Sir Jason tried to pull himself up.

"And she will have," Callie broke into his flow, the lie already on her lips. "She's going to marry Emmet Hadley. Won't that be nice, Papa? You'll have grandchildren and I'll be an aunt."

The effect of Callie's announcement on her father was miraculous. He sank back against the plump down pillows and sighed deeply. "Thank God!" It sounded like a prayer the way he said it. "Now I don't have to worry. Hadley's a good lad with a sizable estate. He'll take care of you girls."

"Perhaps he won't have to," Callie said. "The squire is having a houseful of guests down from London and one of them is an earl. I'll wager that once he sees Diana he'll be bowled over. How would you like an earl for a son-in-law, Papa?"

"Only if he's a good man, Callie." Sir Jason's voice faded slightly. "You girls deserve the very best, especially you, Callie." He reached blindly for her and she grasped his thin hand. "No man could have a better daughter. You're just like your Mama, my darling, darling Rosamund." His eyes slowly closed and he drifted off to sleep, a smile still on his lips at the thought of his wife, dead these past five years of the same fever that had crippled Rosalind.

Callie felt a moment's unreasoning panic until she noticed the even rise and fall of his chest and realized that he was just sleeping. Gently, she laid his frail hand back on the rose-colored comforter and leaned back in the uncomfortable chair, preparing herself for a long vigil.

Her conscience pricked her about the outright lies she had told him, but she didn't really see what else she could have done. Besides, she consoled herself, she hadn't actually told Nanny that Olivia was going to marry Emmet. Nanny had jumped to that conclusion all by herself, and not without justification. Outrage flowed through Callie on her sister's behalf. Nothing could have been clearer than the attentions that Emmet had paid to Olivia on his last leave. And then to jilt her for some unknown Spanish woman! It was just as well Nanny had misinterpreted the situation. She was a tigress where her nurslings were concerned. It was quite within the realms of possibility that Nanny would descend on Emmet and tell him exactly what she thought of such fickle behavior. Callie shuddered at the thought of the scandal that would ensue. It would be a blow to Olivia's pride that she'd never live down.

As for her father, the lie had been necessary, and the morality of it didn't interest Callie in the least. She could hardly comfort her father with their plan to catch Diana a husband. In his present state, he wanted a bird in the hand, not an earl in the bush. Once they had this earl firmly hooked, then they could tell Papa and Nanny that Olivia had changed her mind. It wouldn't seem so important then. Fortunately, with Papa so ill, he wouldn't be meeting anyone to tell about Olivia's supposed engagement, and Nanny prided herself on her refusal to gossip about the family.

- 2 -

"THE PONY CART'S out front, Miss Callie," Price announced from the doorway of the dining room where Callie and Olivia were finishing their breakfast.

"Thank you, Price." Callie set down her tea cup. "Bye, Livy. I'll be back as soon as I find out everything Ada knows about her London visitors."

The shaggy little piebald pony was waiting patiently by the front steps as Callie hurried out into the biting wind. "Poor Nebuchadnezzar," she crooned, rubbing his velvety nose. "I didn't mean to leave you standing out in the wind."

"You didn't, Miss Callie," Thomas, the only groom they employed, assured her. "We just got here. I had the deuce of a time finding the little beast. There's a hole in the west side of the fence, and he'd gotten through and was clean down by the shore by the time I found him."

"A hole!" Callie frowned at Thomas. "But we just had the home paddock refenced completely last summer."

"Yes, miss," Thomas agreed, "but something knocked a section down."

19

"Or some*one*." Callie compressed her lips together in anger. "It was probably the Dale brothers and Albert Talbort smuggling that blessed brandy of theirs."

"I wouldn't be knowing about that, miss," Thomas began.

"Don't lie, Thomas," Callie snapped. "The only one in the whole village who doesn't know that they smuggle brandy is the exciseman from Brighton, and that's only because he considers himself too much above us provincials to ask anyone."

"Yes, miss."

"You tell them, Thomas, that if they can't use the gates like everyone else, I'll make it my business to have a talk with the exciseman."

"If you say so, miss, but. . . ." Thomas clearly didn't like this role as go-between.

"But nothing." Callie climbed into the pony trap. "We haven't got a shilling to spare to fix fences, and, if you don't know it, you should. I simply can't afford to keep replacing fencing."

"I know, Miss Callie." Thomas let go of the pony's bridle and moved back. "I'll stop by the inn tonight. They usually spend their free time there."

"Thank you, Thomas." Callie shook the reins and the pony moved forward at a brisk trot, eager to be off. Callie dismissed the eccentricities of the local smugglers from her mind and breathed in the cold air. Its crispness was reviving her tired mind, and she was grateful. She must learn as much as possible from Ada, and being half-asleep wasn't going to help.

"Aunt Callie? Aunt Callie! I'm talking to you!" The demanding little voice penetrated Callie's thoughts and she looked up, catching sight of Abner Varden, Ada's son, standing beside the narrow road.

"Abner! What are you doing here?" Callie reined in Nebuchadnezzar and gave her attention to the solidly built seven-year-old. "How did you get so far from home?"

"On Brownie. I tied him to a tree down there." He turned

and pointed toward the copse a few hundred yards from the side of the road.

"But your mother..."

"Mama fusses," Abner dismissed the absent Ada. "Aunt Callie, this is important. A matter of life and death!"

"Whose?" Callie firmly pressed her twitching lips together. "Are there spies in the woods?"

"Don't be silly," Abner scoffed. "Spies don't live in woods."

"I stand corrected. Exactly what happened?"

"It's George. He's up a tree!"

"George? Your groom?" Callie hazarded a guess.

"Of course not!" Abner stamped one small foot in exasperation. "I didn't bring a groom. I'm old enough to ride by myself."

"Then who's George?"

"My cat."

"I see." Callie remembered Ada's lamentations about the flea-infested barn cat that one of the grooms had given to Abner the previous week. "Why is he up a tree?"

"Because he climbed it!" Abner obviously was fast losing his patience. "And now he's afraid to come down. Please, Aunt Callie, help him."

One look into Abner's pleading eyes and Callie was lost, despite her private opinion that George would be better left to come down in his own time.

"Well," she temporized, "I guess it wouldn't hurt to take a look at George and his tree."

"Thank you, Aunt Callie." Abner skipped excitedly. "Hurry up. He might fall."

"I doubt it." Callie climbed down from the pony cart and looked around for somewhere to tie the reins. "Cats don't generally fall out of trees."

"George isn't any ordinary cat," Abner protested, and then, noticing her search, asked, "What are you looking for? I told you, George is over there."

"I'm looking for somewhere to tie Nebuchadnezzar's reins so he doesn't wander away."

"Oh, just drop them. He's too fat to go anywhere."

"Insulting a lady's pony is not the way to get her to help you rescue your cat, my lad."

"Then tie him to that bush there." Abner pointed to a scraggly-looking shrub about five feet up the road.

Callie did and then, picking up her skirts so as not to muddy her good dress, followed him into the woods.

"There he is." Abner stopped under a good-sized elm and pointed up into the bare branches.

"There he is all right," Callie agreed, trying to ignore the trusting little face that seemed to think she could solve all problems. Unable to resist Abner's hopeful expression any longer, she finally suggested, "Why don't we try coaxing him out of the tree?"

Abner vetoed the idea. "I did, but he was afraid to come."

Callie looked vaguely around the bare winter landscape as if searching for an inspiration. None came. "Maybe we could find something for him to eat. Then he'd come down. What does he like?"

"Dead rats, dead mice, dead—"

"Never mind," Callie broke into his ghoulish recital. "I get the idea. Here, kitty, kitty," she called on the off chance that he would respond to a different voice. But George was impervious to her plea, remaining perched halfway up the tree.

"If you'll give me a boost, Aunt Callie, I'll climb up and get him. I can't reach the first branch."

"No," Callie refused. "Supposing you fell? You might break your neck, and then where would you be?"

"Dead," Abner replied seriously. "And I'd just as soon not be. Papa's promised me the pick of the spring foals."

"Definitely a compelling reason for staying alive. I'll just have to climb it myself. No one's promised me anything."

"Don't be silly! You can't climb a tree. You're just a girl!" Abner's voice was scathing.

"Ha!" Callie looked down her nose at this small proponent of masculine superiority. "I'll have you know that your mother and I were climbing trees long before you were ever thought of."

"Mama!" Abner obviously couldn't picture his plump mother as a tree climber.

"Yes, your mother. Now sit there, and for heaven's sake, don't say anything. The stupid animal might climb higher if you frighten it."

"George isn't stupid," Abner muttered, although he did sink onto the dead grass under the tree.

Callie leaned back and studied the elm. Despite the fact that she hadn't climbed a tree in well over ten years, she didn't doubt her ability to successfully scale this one. Its limbs were broad and evenly spaced. Taking off her pelisse so that she'd have greater freedom of movement, she tossed it to Abner.

"Be a dear, Abner, and put it in the pony trap please."

She turned back to the tree, jumping for the first limb and catching on with both hands. Wrapping her legs around the first branch, she levered herself up and looked for the next higher limb. Carefully, holding her skirts, she slowly climbed upward, trying not to make any sudden movement for fear of frightening the cat. Finally she reached the branch the cat was sitting on and started to creep stealthily out on the limb. George simply sat there, watching her approach with an unwavering stare.

"Nice kitty, stupid kitty," Callie murmured softly as she reached a hand out toward him. Just when she almost had him in her grasp, he arched his back, emitted an earsplitting howl, and ran straight for her. Instinctively she jerked back, and, to her horror, felt herself slipping. She grabbed frantically, missing the branch and plunging a good five feet before her skirt caught on a broken limb and she hung there like an ornament on a Christmas tree.

"George came down by himself, Aunt Callie, just like you said he would," Abner called up to her. "You can come down now."

"Luck would be a fine thing," Callie muttered, cautiously trying to reach the branch above her, but the sound of her skirt ripping told her that it wasn't going to work. She was well and truly hooked. She couldn't reach the branch above, and, if she ripped her skirt loose, there was no guarantee that she'd be able to catch the one underneath. It was quite possible that she would fall all the way to the ground and break her neck. She remembered her warning to Abner with misgivings.

"Aunt Callie," Abner called up.

"Not now, Abner, I'm thinking."

"That ought to be a novelty," a deep masculine voice observed from directly underneath her.

Horrified, Callie looked down, straight into the gleaming black eyes of a tall, well-built man seated on a huge bay horse. Callie studied him nervously, noting his wind-ruffled black hair, which outlined his lean face and the deep laugh lines etched in his tanned cheeks. Her gaze lingered on his firm lips, which were parted in laughter to reveal perfect white teeth. A superbly tailored coat of olive-green bath superfine covered his broad shoulders, and his snowy neckcloth was tied with a casual elegance that was totally foreign to their small village.

Callie felt a shiver of awareness at his blatant masculinity and could have screamed with frustration at having been caught in such a hoydenish situation. Ignoring her instinctive desire to engage him in conversation, Callie tried to salvage some of her normal dignity.

"Please move on, my good man," she tried in her most supercilious tones.

"Cut line, madam. Those haughty airs don't go with all the leg you're showing."

"How dare you!" Callie shouted and quieted quickly as she heard her dress rip still further.

"When you get to know me better, you'll find that I'll dare most anything," he said.

"Contrary to your beliefs—" Callie began and then broke off as he dismounted and walked to the base of the tree. "What are you doing?" she demanded as he reached up and grabbed the first branch with no trouble.

"I'm coming up to rescue you, of course." He swung himself competently up.

"But, but, you can't," she wailed. "My skirt is caught, and . . ." She trailed off into embarrassed silence.

"Good God, madam, I've seen women in their undergarments before. Besides," he continued, ignoring her strangled gasp, "I read all the King Arthur legends when I was a boy, and I always wanted to rescue a maiden in distress."

"Sir Galahad himself," Callie sneered, envying the ease with which he scaled the tree.

"No, Galahad was a fool. Only a complete block would worship a woman from afar all those years."

"His love was pure and undefiled by the flesh!" Callie defended the maligned knight hotly.

"There speaks a virgin or a wife with a singularly inept husband."

"How dare you!"

"You've already asked me that. Try not to repeat yourself." He stood on the branch right below the one she was hanging on. "Now," his voice became brisk, "I'm standing right behind you about even with your . . ." He paused, cleared his throat and then continued. "I'm going to inch out along this branch. When I get closer to you, put your arms around my neck, then I'll rip your skirt off the tree. Understand?"

"Yes," Callie grated, furious at the cat for putting her in such an embarrassing position, furious with the stranger for relishing it, but most of all, furious with herself for ever having climbed the tree in the first place.

"Now." His voice was immediately behind her.

Callie's breath caught in her lungs as his hard hands encircled her waist and turned her around. After one quick look into his twinkling eyes, she lowered her gaze hastily, concentrating on the pristine whiteness of his neckcloth.

"Hold on," he ordered, and she put her arms around his neck obediently, trying to ignore the sensual roughness of his jaw as her hand brushed it. "Tighter."

Expelling her breath in annoyance, Callie tightened her grip until it resembled a stranglehold, and then immediately regretted her impulsive action as the intimate contact with his body made her skin tingle and quickened her pulse.

"Excellent," he approved: "I like a woman who can take orders."

Callie's sense of humor surfaced, and she bit down on a giggle that threatened to escape, then frantically loosened her hold.

"Now to unfasten your dress." One slight yank and the cloth separated. "I'm going to back up slowly. When we reach the crotch of the tree, I'll put you down."

Callie nodded, trying to shut her mind to the feel and smell of the stranger, but it proved impossible. Her small, cold nose was pressed up against his shirt and the odor of fresh linen, soap, and the more elusive, slightly musky aroma of his skin filled her nostrils. Her breasts tingled where they were pressed against his chest, and her lower body shivered with reaction to the feel of his hard-muscled thighs pressing into her soft flesh.

Once they reached the main branch, he lowered Callie onto the limb and helped her to hold on.

"Can you climb down by yourself?" he inquired.

"Of course I can." Callie sniffed. "I'm not made of such poor stuff as that."

"Very well. I'll go first and you follow."

"But you can't," she protested. "I mean . . ."

"You mean that I'll see your very pretty undergarments." His voice was threaded with laughter. "But I've already seen them. Besides, it's safest. That way, if you fall, I can catch you." He paused. "Of course, if you'd rather I carried you down . . ." He moved toward her.

"No!" Callie shrank back against the tree limb. "I'll follow."

"A wise decision." He flicked her cheek carelessly with a hard finger. "It's always best to admit your limitations."

"Limitations!" Callie sputtered.

"Limitations," he repeated. "To paraphrase your young friend down there, you're nothing but a girl."

"I happen to like being a girl!"

"I'm sure you do, but this is hardly the place to flirt with me. Wait until we're on the ground, and then I'll be happy to oblige you."

Callie closed her eyes and swallowed a furious retort, realizing how foolish it was to rise to his bating. "If you will start now," she forced out in level tones.

Skillfully, he started the downward climb, waiting patiently on each branch for her to follow him. Finally he reached the last limb and dropped to the ground.

"Hang onto that branch and I'll catch you," he called up to her.

"That won't be necessary. I can jump."

"Don't be so damned stubborn, madam. I haven't the time to cope with any broken bones just because you've taken umbrage."

There was a certain amount of truth in what he'd said and Callie was honest enough to admit it. Giving way to the inevitable, she slowly lowered herself. Hard hands grabbed her waist and she was swung gently to the ground.

Callie turned hastily to face him, hiding her ripped skirt.

"Thank you very much," Callie began, aiming her thanks at his silk waistcoat, unable to face the amusement in his eyes.

"Aunt Callie," Abner interrupted her, "I can see your shift. You shouldn't wear clothes with holes in them."

"Abner Varden!" Callie swung around, realizing, the moment she heard the man's laughter, that it had been a mistake.

"Never correct a lady, young man," he instructed Abner.

"Oh, she's not a lady, mister. She's just my Aunt Callie."

"I'm honored to meet you, my Aunt Callie." The man took her limp left hand—the right one was clutching the remains of her skirt together—and executed a graceful bow over it.

"I'm not my Aunt Callie. I mean you're not my Aunt Callie. Oh, go away, do!" Callie yanked her hand free and glared at the man.

"All right," Abner said, clutching George closer to his muddy, brown nankeen jacket, "if you're going to yell, I will. I don't know what you're so mad about anyway, Aunt

Callie. George came down by himself. You didn't have to rescue him. 'Bye." Abner held the cat closer, ignoring the animal's abortive attempts to escape, and started jogging toward the patiently waiting Brownie.

"Thank you very much for your assistance, sir." Callie gave the tall stranger a dismissing nod of her head, but unfortunately he didn't move.

"You mean I don't get to keep you?" The man sounded surprised. "In fairy tales, when the knight rescued the maiden in distress, he always got to keep her."

"I may have been a maiden in distress, but you aren't any knight." Callie turned a smoldering eye on him. "And I'll thank you to quit making a May game out of me and go away!"

"But I can't do that," he replied, leaning nonchalantly up against the tree trunk. "Now that I've rescued you, I feel a certain responsibility for you."

"My dear sir, I am perfectly capable of seeing myself home." Callie gathered up her shredded skirt and started toward the road, intent on escaping. "I have my pony cart right by the side of the road."

The man grabbed the bay's reins and started after her.

"My name is—"

"No!" Callie interrupted him, not wanting to know if the elegant stranger really was, as she was beginning to suspect, the Earl of Rutledge. She preferred to postpone finding out. She just couldn't accept any more complications today.

The tall man quirked a sable eyebrow and gave her a curiously penetrating look. "An original guess, but not very accurate."

"I wasn't guessing." Callie speeded up slightly. "I simply don't want to know."

"Now, that's not very polite," he pointed out, "after I went so far out of my way to rescue you. We men of fashion are not used to all this exercise."

Callie paused and regarded him thoughtfully, her chagrin momentarily eclipsed by curiosity about the man. "I don't know exactly what you are, but it's obvious that you aren't a dandy. You haven't a single watch, fob, or quizzing glass to your name." She started walking again.

"Quizzing glasses are usually relegated to the drawing room."

"And you weren't even breathing hard after you climbed that tree," Callie continued as if he hadn't spoken. "So whatever else you are, you're used to physical activity."

"Any other conclusions?"

"Yes. Your tailor doesn't come from around here. Were you on your way to Brighton and got lost?"

"Sorry, my dear, you're out on that one." He paused as they reached the side of the road. "Where's this pony trap of yours?"

"Right—" Callie turned and glanced around, thinking she must have entered the woods farther down, but the road was discouragingly blank in both directions. "But he was here. I tied him to a bush over there."

"Hmm." The man walked along the side of the road in the direction she had pointed, looking along the ground, the big bay following close behind. "Here's where your bush was." He pointed to some loose dirt. "He must have simply pulled it out."

"That wretched beast!" Callie felt like crying in vexation. "The only loyalty that animal has is to his stomach. He's probably home by now, eating his fill."

"And where is home?" the man asked.

"Oh, a few miles down the road," Callie answered vaguely. "I can walk it easily. Thank you again for your help. I won't keep you any longer."

"There's no need to be afraid of me, Aunt Callie," he said, sounding highly amused. "I have no intention of attacking you just because we're in a lonely, deserted spot."

Callie blushed scarlet at his blunt words, but refused to back down. "That's perfectly obvious!" she snapped.

"You intrigue me. Why should it be obvious?"

"My dear sir, one has only to look at you to see that you're a wealthy man. You can well afford a mistress. Besides, I'm hardly the type of woman to inspire lusting thoughts in any man, especially one as sophisticated as you."

"Hmmm." He eyed her with deceptive casualness.

"So, if you will leave," Callie suggested pointedly as she crushed a momentary disappointment that he didn't at least claim to find her attractive.

"It's definitely time to be off," he agreed, swinging himself into the saddle. "You're going to catch an inflammation of the lungs with the wind whistling through your skirts."

Silently, Callie turned her back on him and started up the road. She heard the sound of a bay's hooves, but she was totally unprepared when the horse stopped behind her and an iron-hard arm circled her waist, lifting her effortlessly into the saddle.

"Put me down!" she demanded, infuriated at his high-handedness, but his arm merely tightened and she found herself crushed against his chest. Her frantic movements served only to heighten her awareness of the hard muscles barely hidden by his fashionable coat. The warmth of his large hand spread over her rib cage penetrated the fine wool of her dress and seemed to squeeze the breath from her lungs. She was appalled by her reaction to him. It was fright because he was behaving in such an autocratic manner, she assured herself, trying hard to believe it. Unfortunately, Callie had never been very good at self-deception, and she acknowledged that, while her mind might have reservations about the stranger, her body had no such inhibitions.

Nervously, she licked dry lips and forced herself to relax, worried that he might pick up her agitation and guess its cause. Immediately his grasp loosened until he was merely holding her securely in place.

"You've learned your first lesson, Aunt Callie. I will not tolerate opposition. You'd do well to remember it. Now, where is your home?"

"Straight ahead," Callie whispered, staring down at the large hands that held the bay's reins.

"Look at me, madam!" he snapped.

Much as it grated to obey, she did, realizing that she was in no position to argue.

"I have no intention of hurting you, my dear," he continued in a softer tone, "but neither do I intend to leave you on a deserted road miles from home in your state of deshabille."

Callie searched his warm black eyes for a sign of an ulterior motive, but they only looked politely back at her. Quite obviously her own physical awareness of him was not reciprocated. There was no sign in his words or manner that he found holding her any more exciting than he would have found holding Abner. It was his undeniable lack of interest that stiffened her pride, and she managed to respond normally.

"Thank you for your consideration, sir."

"You're welcome, my dear." He accepted her words at face value and, gathering her shivering body closer to him, nudged the bay into a swift canter. "You're half-frozen."

"I put my pelisse in the cart before I went up for that wretched beast," Callie explained.

"Poor Aunt Callie. George is better able to take care of himself than you are."

"That's not true! I'm not some little die-away miss. I'll have you know that I'm five-and-twenty and have been running our estate for years."

"A veritable Amazon." He chuckled. "And whose estate is it?"

"Papa's," Callie admitted grudgingly. "He doesn't have any sons."

"Nor sons-in-law?"

"No," she answered shortly. This was dangerous ground, and she didn't want to discuss it. Despite her fears that he might pursue the subject, he lapsed into silence. A silence Callie was happy not to break. She had no desire to engage in social repartee with the man. It was glaringly obvious that he was far outside her league. She allowed her body to relax against his and simply enjoyed the sensation of being held closely to him.

"Stop here," Callie instructed, jerking herself out of her introspective thoughts. "I live in that house." She pointed down the graceful avenue of oak trees that formed a tunnel leading to the house. "No, please," she protested as he started up the driveway. "Put me down here. It'll be hard enough to explain my ripped dress, let alone a strange man."

"You won't find yourself in trouble, will you?" He frowned down into her worried face. "Perhaps I better come in and—"

"Oh, no, you don't understand. Papa would never mind an accident, but he's very ill and mustn't be worried."

"And you think I might worry him?" he inquired, making no attempt to help her down.

"Not if you keep talking about Arthur and his knights." Callie gurgled with laughter. "He'd be so pleased to find another man who reads that he'd never think to ask where I found you. All the men around here care about are hunting and crops, in that order. It's my sisters who'd be curious, and, since none of this morning's events reflect well on me, I'd just as soon not have to explain them."

"There's nothing wrong with having a warm heart, my dear." He stroked a gentle finger down the side of her cheek. "But next time, temper it with common sense."

Seeming to lose interest in the conversation, the man swung down from the saddle. He reached up for her and set her carefully on the ground. "Run along, Aunt Callie." He turned her toward the house and gave her a gentle push. "I'll wait here until you get inside."

Picking up her skirts, Callie raced down the deserted driveway and around the side of the house, intent on sneaking in through the library door so that she could reach her room and change her dress before anyone saw her. The last glimpse she had of him was astride the magnificent bay, patiently watching her.

She let herself into the small side door that opened into the library and looked around the room with a chill of foreboding. This was her father's retreat. Usually there was a blazing fire in the grate and Sir Jason could be found behind the huge carved mahogany library table which stood in front of the ceiling to floor windows on the north wall. Today the fireplace was cold and empty and the wine-colored drapes were closed tightly, giving the room a deserted, mourning look. Determinedly, Callie rejected her fanciful imaginings.

Her father was going to get better. He had to. By this time next month he'd be back at his desk eagerly writing his Shakespearean opus, she told herself.

Callie opened the library door and peered into the hallway. A quick look in either direction was sufficient to assure her that no one was about, and, gathering up her torn skirts, she sprinted for the back staircase, taking the steps two at a time. Once on the second floor, she tiptoed so as not to disturb her father if he should be asleep.

Ten minutes later, she was attired conventionally in a plain blue woolen dress which, while covering her adequately, did nothing to improve her looks. That didn't bother her in the slightest. She had long ago admitted her lack of looks.

"Oh, Miss Callie." Price's worried whisper halted her on the third step from the bottom.

"What's the matter, Price?" Callie ran down the remaining stairs and grabbed the old man's immaculate sleeve. "Papa?"

"Oh, no, Miss Callie," he hastened to reassure her. "I didn't mean to worry you. It's just that the vicar's arrived and he's demanding to see Sir Jason. I put him in the morning room, but—"

"You did exactly right," Callie said. "Never mind about our dear vicar. I'll take care of him. Where are my sisters?"

"Miss Olivia's sitting with Sir Jason, and Miss Rosalind is resting. I think all this worry has made her leg ache."

"And Diana?"

"Miss Diana is in the sewing room. She said that nothing on earth would induce her to sit with the vicar."

"Hmm," Callie murmured noncommittally. "Well, I'd best see the man. Oh, Price," Callie called after him as he started down the hall, "please find out if Nebuchadnezzar has returned. And if he has, have him brought around to the front again. I got out of the cart and he bolted."

"I'll send someone over to the stables right this minute, Miss Callie. Don't you worry none. That beast's a real homebody." And with this bit of reassurance, Price shuffled off toward the kitchens.

Callie gave an enormous yawn, then mentally braced herself for the meeting with the vicar.

Despite the fact that it was Callie's nature to like people, she had never been able to work up one iota of enthusiasm for Phineas Marston. She had disliked him the first time she had seen him six months ago, and closer acquaintance had served only to harden her feelings.

"Reverend Marston," Callie greeted him from the doorway. "How kind of you to call."

"I came as soon as I heard the bad news." He hoisted his hefty bulk out of the shabby wing chair. "I felt it my Christian duty to comfort you in your hour of need."

He sounded just like a character out of a Gothic novel, Callie thought with a flash of surprise. But what seemed right and natural in a book sounded ludicrous in reality.

"How kind of you," Callie clipped out. "Please be seated." Callie studied him openly as she crossed the wide expanse of worn Wilton carpeting and sat down in an armchair opposite him. He was about as tall as the stranger had been, but here the resemblance ended. Beside the stranger, Phineas Marston was a caricature of a gentleman. His rusty black coat fit like a mitten instead of a glove, and his elaborately tied neckcloth was a dingy gray decorated with a few yellow spots from his last meal, Callie noted with disgust. His skin-tight buckskins only accentuated his paunch, and his hessians were smudged instead of gleaming, like the stranger's.

"I told that old fool who opened the door to take me up to Sir Jason, but he was confused and put me in here."

"Our butler's name is Price, and he wasn't the least bit confused. He was merely following orders like the excellent servant he is. I told him that no one was allowed to visit Papa."

"But surely," Marston spread his pudgy fingers with their dirt-encrusted nails, "that doesn't include a man of God?"

"My father already has God with him. What need has he of a go-between?"

"Now, now, Miss Callie." He smiled patronizingly at

her. "If you were a man, that would be blasphemy. You shouldn't say such things."

"Oh? Don't you believe that God is everywhere?"

"Yes, of course, but—"

"And if God is everywhere, then He's in Papa's room. So don't you feel it an impertinence to interrupt Him?"

"I—"

"Which is just as well," Callie continued undaunted, "because I refuse to allow anyone to see him."

"You poor child," the vicar sympathized, "having to take the burden of this estate on your own shoulders. You need a man to help you." Callie shivered inwardly as she glimpsed the momentary greed that lit his beady brown eyes. "I imagine you'll inherit The Meadings since you're the eldest?" His avaricious gaze swept around the room.

So that was it! Callie could have laughed had the situation not been so desperate. Phineas Marston was imagining himself as the master of Meadings!

"You imagine wrong, Reverend Marston. The estate's entailed."

"Entailed!" He jerked upright with shock.

"Yes," Callie continued, "my cousin Gilmer inherits everything."

"Everything?" he repeated, hope dying hard.

"Everything. My sisters and I will be left virtually penniless." Callie drove the final nail in the coffin of his ambition.

"I see, I'm sure, I mean—" he blustered.

"I know exactly what you mean." Callie smiled blandly at his attempt to disassociate himself from their dilemma. "And I appreciate your coming out to visit Papa. Perhaps next time you come he'll be up."

"Yes, yes." He shifted uncertainly.

"Will you be stopping by to visit the squire's on the way back?" Callie hopefully threw out the red herring.

"Squire Varden's." He frowned slightly. "Is anyone there sick?"

"Oh, no." Callie felt a momentary twinge of guilt for

what she was about to do to Ada, but she ignored it. All Ada had to worry about was the baby's teething. Ada was much better able to cope with the Reverend Marston than she. "Haven't you heard?" Callie paused for effect. "They have visitors down from London, and one of them is an earl."

"An earl!" The vicar leaned forward eagerly. "Which one?"

"Rutledge. Do you know him?"

"Of him. He has huge estates in Northumberland and Wales. He must have fifty livings to appoint."

"Really?"

Callie almost laughed at the calculating expression on his face.

"Yes, indeed, a very powerful man is the earl, very powerful."

"But not in the eyes of the Lord," Callie threw in with pious self-righteousness. "In His eyes all men are equal."

"Yes, yes, so they are and, since you won't let me visit poor Sir Jason, I won't be keeping you."

"Of course not, Reverend Marston."

- 3 -

THIRTY MINUTES LATER, Callie approached Ada's with trepidation. Although she tried to believe the stranger she had met earlier was *not* the Earl of Rutledge, common sense told her that there really was no other explanation. There were no signs of any guests about the stately red-brick house, though, and Callie cherished the thought that the London visitors might not yet have arrived.

A gardener working on the boxwood hedge that grew in front of the house dropped his tool when he saw Callie and hurried over to the pony trap. "Good morning, miss," he greeted her respectfully, tugging the brim of the blue cap he was wearing. "Shall I take the little beastie around to the stables?"

"Yes, please. I'll be awhile, and I'd be grateful if you'd find him a warm spot out of the wind."

"A pleasure, miss." He bobbed his head and moved toward Nebuchadnezzar's head.

"I don't believe I've met you," Callie said as she climbed down from the pony trap.

"I be Evens, miss. Come down from London to help lay out the gardens for the squire."

"How nice. I'll look forward to seeing the results. Gardening this close to the sea can be a trial. Nothing much seems to flourish."

"You wait and see," Evens promised before leading the pony toward the stables.

Dismissing the new gardener, Callie hurried up the three broad, granite steps to the front door. Before she had a chance to rap the gleaming lion-shaped knocker, the heavy oak door swung inward.

"Good morning, Miss Callie. It's a pleasure to see you."

"Good morning, Johnston. Is Mrs. Varden receiving visitors?"

"Yes, miss. She's in the back parlor." He held out his hand for her pelisse and gloves. "I'm glad to hear that your father is so much improved today."

"Thank you." Callie accepted his words without even wondering how he had found that out. Long ago she had learned that the most efficient spy network in the country was comprised of servants. They seemed to know things long before the individuals involved did.

Ada Varden was sitting in the back parlor, her hands curled round a steaming cup of tea and an expression of what could only be called beatific satisfaction on her plump face.

"You look like a cat that just discovered a pot of cream," Callie observed as she walked into the room.

"Callie!" Ada squeaked and beamed at her friend. "You frightened me."

"I would think that just sitting in this room would frighten you," Callie replied dryly as she looked around in disgust.

Ada had had the room refurbished in the latest style after returning from her annual fortnight stay in London last spring. Now crocodile-legged couches vied for attention with lion-legged rosewood chairs.

"It is rather overpowering," Ada agreed, "but, I assure you, it's all the crack. Everyone in London was having their drawing rooms done over in the Egyptian motif."

"Perhaps, but I still liked it better before." Callie sat down on a crocodile-legged rosewood chair upholstered in olive-green and brass stripes. "What's that?" She peered curiously at the strange-looking contraption on an Egyptian writing table, which was supported by four brass sphinxes and decorated with gilded Egyptian hieroglyphics.

"It's an oil lamp," Ada told her without enthusiasm. "It burns some kind of oil that smells just like dead fish. Tristam brought it down from London. He says they're all the rage."

"Considering some of the things that are all the rage among the *haut ton,* I hardly consider that a recommendation," Callie observed tartly. "But never mind about Tristam and his toys. Tell me," Callie leaned eagerly toward Ada, "is it true?"

"Yes." Ada had no need to ask what Callie was talking about. "It's true." She almost wriggled with excitement.

"A real earl?"

"Yes, the Earl of Rutledge. He's ever so handsome—"

"You mean he's already here?" Callie interrupted anxiously.

"Oh yes. They all came down from London together yesterday evening."

"What does the earl look like?" Callie asked as nonchalantly as she could, praying that he had blond hair and blue eyes.

"As I said, he's quite handsome," Ada rhapsodized. "Everything prime about him. Curly black hair, black eyes, broad shoulders, and I'm sure they're his and not due simply to his tailor's skill."

Callie sank back in her chair, her last hope gone.

"You're not looking all the thing, Callie," Ada observed. "May I pour you out a cup of tea? It's fresh."

"I'd love some." Callie struggled to sound normal. "That wind out there is bitter cold."

"I'm sorry," Ada apologized, hastening to pour the tea. "I should have asked you at once, but I swear I'm in such a dither. I think I could almost forgive Tristam all the money he's cost my poor Gervais, though. We've never had such distinguished visitors."

Callie pushed aside the worries of the effect her unseemly behavior probably had had on one of those "distinguished visitors." It was possible that once the earl saw Diana's captivating beauty, he would forget about the scrape Callie had gotten into.

"Um, Ada," Callie fumbled for the right words, "this earl. Is he really rich? I mean your nephew . . ." Her voice trailed off.

"You mean how did a ne'er-do-well like Tristam come to know him?" Ada was too excited by her guests to take umbrage at Callie's implied insult. "Actually Tristam doesn't know the earl all that well. Tristam's friend is the earl's nephew and ward, James Kershaw. It seems that Mr. Kershaw has been sick this winter with an inflammation of the lungs and his physician recommended the sea air. The earl was going to take him to Brighton, but Tristam invited him here instead."

"And the earl came along to watch over his ward?"

"That's right. But what does it matter why he came? He's here."

"How old is this ward?"

"Oh, Tristam's age, I think. About twenty-one or twenty-two. Why?"

"Just curious." Callie dismissed the ward as too young for Olivia. "And Rutledge really is wealthy?" Callie persisted.

"Oh, yes." Ada leaned forward, eager to share her information. "He's one of the wealthiest men in England. Seventy-five thousand a year and huge estates in Northumberland and Wales."

"And he isn't married or engaged?"

"No." Ada shook her head. "He's rarely in London, so no one has had a chance to snaffle him. Why?"

Callie took a swift look toward the door to make sure there were no servants listening, and then whispered, "Because we intend to try to get him for Diana."

"Diana!" Ada gasped.

"Don't sound so flummoxed, Ada. Diana may not have

a portion, but her lineage is impeccable, and she's certainly beautiful enough."

"Of course she is," Ada hastened to agree. "She's one of the loveliest girls I've ever seen. Why, if she were in London, she'd be an instant success." Ada warmed to her theme. "Perhaps, when your father is better?"

"There isn't any money for a London season," Callie said flatly. "We've got to find her a husband now. Poor Papa is worrying himself into another seizure thinking about what's going to happen to us after he dies."

"And well he should!" For once Ada lost her good humor. "He has to know that Joan Sutcliff will evict you the moment Gilmer inherits. Your father should have made an effort to have found you and Olivia suitable husbands years ago." Ada flushed and then hurried on when she suddenly remembered the heartbreak that Sir Jason's one attempt at matchmaking had caused Callie. "Unless Olivia means to have Emmet despite his having lost an arm?"

"Olivia and Emmet regard each other as brother and sister," Callie lied, having no illusions about Ada's ability to keep a secret.

"That's a shame." Ada shook her head regretfully. "He has such a tidy little property, too, but if it isn't to be, it isn't to be. We'll capture the earl instead."

"I hope so," Callie said. "It's not an impossible task. If he isn't even used to London society, Diana's beauty should stun him. After all, what else is there for him to do in Kent at this time of year?"

"True." Ada fell in with Callie's plans as she'd been doing all her life. "But we might have a problem with one of the other guests."

"Other guests?" Callie asked. "Rosalind was so full of Rutledge that I forgot to ask if there were any others."

"Oh, yes, indeed. Tristam invited some others so that they could help entertain each other. There's d'Armagnac and Charles and Dorcas Parr."

"A Frenchman?"

"He works for the Horse Guards in London. His family

came over during the Terror and when we finally beat Boney, he says he'll go back. He's the heir to some title or other, but I can't remember which. I never could keep all those Frenchies straight."

"And the Parrs?" Callie prompted.

"That's where we're going to have trouble," Ada admitted. "When Mrs. Parr heard that the Earl of Rutledge was coming, she asked Tristam to invite her and her husband, too. And she'd only met Tristam the week before at some party."

"Are you sure she knows the earl? If he's rarely in London..."

"She knows him, all right. Her husband has an estate near Rutledge in Northumberland. And, besides, if you'd have seen her hanging over him last night..." Ada clicked her tongue in exasperation. "It was disgusting!"

"But what about her husband? Surely he won't allow his wife to flirt with another man right under his very nose."

"Bah! He's an old fool. He must be sixty if he's a day, and she can't be much older than we are. Mr. Parr fell asleep over his port and never even came into the drawing room to see what his wife was up to."

"Perhaps the earl will discourage her himself?" Callie asked.

"Not likely." Ada disabused her of the idea. "I've never met a man yet who didn't lap up a woman's attentions. Any woman's, let alone one as beautiful as Dorcas Parr."

"She's beautiful?"

"Exquisite, much as it pains me to admit it. She has gorgeous black hair, big brown eyes, a perfect complexion, and her figure..." Ada shook her head at the unfairness of it all. "She's shaped perfectly, without a blemish on her, and there's no doubt about it because the dress she was wearing left nothing to the imagination."

"Oh, dear!" Callie leaned back in her chair and rubbed her aching forehead. "I have the horrible feeling that this is going to be even harder than I thought."

"Things usually are," Ada agreed, "but we'll manage. We always have."

"We've got to!" Callie convulsively clutched her fist. "It doesn't matter so much about me," she rushed on. "I could always find some way to make out. But the others. Olivia and Diana haven't a clue about how to go on. They need protecting. And little Rosalind...I just can't bear the thought of Joan turning her into a slave for that frog-faced daughter of hers."

"Don't you worry, Callie. Rutledge will never know what happened to him. A man doesn't stand a chance against a really determined woman, let alone four of us. We'll have him caught and the notice in the *Gazette* before he ever realizes the danger."

"What's he like?"

"A real top-sawyer, a—"

"You've already told me what he looks like," Callie broke into Ada's rhapsodies. "If you keep going on about how irresistible he is, I'll begin to suspect you of harboring a secret passion for the man."

Ada seemed to give serious consideration to Callie's teasing. "No, I don't think so. I'll stick to my Gervais, thank you. He may not be as handsome as the earl, but he's easygoing, and I can read him like a book. I doubt if Rutledge's own mother could tell what he's thinking behind that polite mask he presents to the world."

"You mean he's hard?" Callie asked in dismay.

"No," Ada answered somewhat uncertainly. "But I think he could be if he wanted. Oh, I'm not sure what I do mean, Callie. I've never met anyone like him before."

"Perhaps he's just bored?" Callie suggested.

"Thanks for your confidence in my abilities as a hostess." Ada giggled. "But you could well be right. He was up and down for breakfast at seven."

"Seven! I thought all peers slept till noon."

"Not in the country, although I will admit I was a little surprised to see him down that early. I was only up because poor little Mary is teething."

"Is he around now?" Callie looked nervously toward the door. "I'd really rather not meet him yet."

"Oh, no." Ada put her mind to rest. "Right after breakfast

he went for a ride." Callie stiffened slightly. "He said he wouldn't be back until luncheon."

"What about the others?"

"Asleep," Ada dismissed them. "Tristam never did rise early, and James Kershaw is supposed to rest as much as possible. Mrs. Parr's maid says that she never gets up before one." Ada noticed her friend's empty cup. "Would you like some more tea?"

"Yes, please."

"Would you like to bring Diana to dinner tomorrow?" Ada asked. "That way you can meet the earl and put your plan into action."

"I haven't got a plan yet. I'm going to go over a novel this afternoon. I know they're hardly true to life, but on the other hand, they undoubtedly contain a kernel of truth somewhere in them. All I have to do is to separate the fact from the fiction. Maybe it would be best to introduce Diana to him at a ball," Callie mused. "She could be wearing some lovely creation and sweep him off his feet."

"Yes, but it would take days to arrange a ball. We'd best not waste the time. He could leave, despite his nephew," Ada pointed out.

"True," Callie conceded. "It was just an idea, anyway. And you're right about a ball's taking too much time. Once he notices what a good housekeeper you are, he's liable to feel safe in leaving the boy in your care."

"Maybe I could slip up a little." Ada giggled. "Like sending up cold shaving water or dampening his sheets."

"With my luck, he'd simply decide to remove his wretched nephew."

"He's not wretched," Ada contradicted her. "He's a very sweet boy, gentle and thoughtful. I simply can't understand why he's a friend of Tristam's."

"Perhaps under all that gentleness he yearns to be adventuresome like Tristam."

"Foolhardy, more likely!" Ada snapped. "If you knew his latest start—" Ada stopped and clamped her lips together. "I'm sorry, Callie, you've enough on your plate without me burdening you with tales about Tristam."

"He's still young yet," Callie tried to comfort her friend. "When he grows up..."

"Perhaps." Clearly Ada had her doubts. "At any rate, will you come tomorrow night?"

"Yes, I think so. The sooner we get started the better. You wouldn't happen to know Rutledge's favorite color, would you?"

"From the way he was hanging over Mrs. Parr last night, I'd say flesh tones!"

"At least skin is cheap," Callie retorted, then erupted into gales of laughter. Calming herself after a few moments and wiping her eyes, she set down the empty teacup. "I'd best be going. If we're coming to dinner tomorrow, I'll need to see about a dress for Diana. And I want to read through *Isabella's Quest* for ideas on ensnaring the unwary male."

Ada stood up with Callie and walked her to the front door, where a paternal Johnston handed Callie her pelisse and gloves.

"I'll see you tomorrow night." Ada kissed Callie's cheek. "Don't forget."

"It's not very likely," Callie said dryly, "considering that our whole future is at stake. Bless you for your help, Ada. You're a true friend." Callie gave her a quick hug and then slipped through the door, closing it quietly behind her.

Callie looked around for the gardener, but he wasn't to be seen. She was about to go and fetch the pony trap herself when she saw Nebuchadnezzer rounding the corner of the house, a small stableboy driving him. The lad steered him to the steps and stopped with a flourish before climbing down.

"You certainly drove him to an inch," Callie praised the boy and smiled inwardly as he visibly swelled at her words.

"Than'ee, miss." He tugged his forelock and backed away.

Callie climbed into the trap and started the stolid pony with a slap of the reins, then waved good-bye to the stableboy. Once on the road, she settled back onto the hard wooden seat and considered what she'd learned from Ada. Not much, she had to admit, other than the fact that Rutledge appealed physically to Ada. And, she admitted honestly, he appealed to her, too.

Hopefully he wasn't a rake, though. Callie thought with misgivings of the man she had met. She didn't know what she'd do if he turned out to have libertine propensities. How could she possibly urge her naïve sister to marry him then? But if she didn't, there was a very good chance that Diana would wind up as some man's mistress. The problem chased itself around her head in a never-ending circle and she turned at the sound of a horse's hooves, grateful for the interruption to her frantic thoughts.

A lone rider was crossing the standing rubble in the hay field to her right. Thoughtfully she squinted, trying to make out the rider. Emmet Hadley. She recognized him when he was halfway across the field. He was dressed in a somber brown coat, his empty right sleeve pinned to his side. The horse was a very old beast who moved more like a rocking horse than one of the highly-spirited animals Emmet had been wont to ride before he lost his arm.

He's having to learn how to balance himself all over again, Callie realized with a burst of pity for the tall, slender young man. But the pity died almost immediately as she remembered her jilted sister. Briefly she debated ignoring him and riding on, but, much as she wanted to snub him, she suppressed the impulse. There could be only one reason to ignore a friend she had grown up with, and that would be because Olivia was upset by his defection. She owed it to Olivia's pride to pretend that absolutely nothing had changed, that Olivia had never considered him to be more than a childhood friend. So Callie pinned an insincere smile on her face and waited for Emmet to catch up with her.

"Callie, I wanted to ask after your father," Emmet began, pulling the placid animal to a halt.

"Papa is much improved today." Callie's voice was stilted. "Dr. Adams feels that he'll recover fully in time."

"What's wrong, Callie?" Emmet's bitter voice sounded loud in the still air. "Don't you feel comfortable talking to a cripple?"

"Your body isn't the only thing that's crippled, Emmet

Hadley!" Callie retorted. "Your mind is, too, to say nothing of your sense of honor. If you can't talk to people without reading self-pitying motives into everything they say, then stay home and become a recluse! Good afternoon!" Callie jerked the reins, and the startled pony lunged forward into a trot, leaving Emmet standing by the side of the road in pathetic dignity.

Callie hadn't gone a hundred yards before she was bitterly sorry for her hasty words. Emmet had endured a lot recently, and despite his harsh tone, he was still her friend. It hurt to see him so desperately defensive. Not even for what he had done to Olivia did Callie want him to suffer anything else. She looked back, uncertain of what to do, but Emmet had turned his horse around and was making his cautious way back home. Callie shook her head wearily. She just couldn't handle any more problems now, she tried to tell herself. But Emmet Hadley's twisted, bitter face kept getting between the truth of what she was saying and her soft heart.

- 4 -

"WHAT DO YOU THINK, Callie?" Diana turned from the mirror hesitantly and faced her sister.

"Perfect, absolutely perfect!" Callie breathed a thankful sigh of relief at the exquisite picture Diana presented. Her white crepe dress had a square neckline and tiny puffed sleeves trimmed with pale pink velvet ribbons. Matching ribbons caught the gown just under her bosom before the skirt fell straight to the floor.

"I wish we could have had real pink roses for your hair." Callie reached up and repositioned one of the pink silk roses in the circlet which confined Diana's golden curls. "But, at this time of year, the nearest real roses would be in Brighton and they'd cost the earth."

"Oh, Callie, I'm so frightened." Diana's lips trembled.

"There's no need to be," Callie insisted. "You look like a dream come to life. Now we'd best find Livy and be on our way. We don't want to be late."

They found Olivia in her room, trying to coax a wayward curl into place.

"Try wetting it, Livy," Diana suggested. "That usually helps."

"Oh, what difference does it make!" Olivia snapped.

"You're right." Callie deliberately misunderstood her sister's words. "You look slap up to the echo. That pale blue silk exactly matches your eyes, and those tiny puffed sleeves are all the crack."

"Which is more than can be said for you. You look like a quiz with that plain navy georgette and your hair all skinned back into a bun. It doesn't even fit you right," Olivia disparaged the gown. "The bodice hangs and it's too short."

"Thank you for the kind words." Callie swallowed her anger. "I know you wanted a new dress, Livy, but there was barely time to get one made for Diana. At least you had a perfectly good evening gown left from last season and weren't reduced to wearing one of Mama's old ones."

"It's not my fault that you never like to go to parties!" Olivia grabbed her sky-blue shawl and flounced out the door.

"I don't think you look too bad, Callie," Diana offered hesitantly. "Just kind of... of..." Her voice trailed off.

"Sober? Matronly?" Callie laughed with wry humor. "Actually, that's exactly why I chose it, Diana. I wanted to appear as inconspicuous as possible. That way you'll look all the more ravishing by comparison. Try not to mind Livy too much, Diana. She still hasn't gotten over Emmet's defection."

"The poor dear." The tenderhearted Diana forgave Olivia's temperament.

They caught up with Olivia in the front hall and hurried out through the heavy oak door. Thomas was patiently standing beside the two brown horses, his shoulders hunched against the wind.

"Evening," he greeted them as he opened the door to the landaulet and let down the steps. "Nasty night, isn't it? The sea's running fair high."

"It certainly is." Callie waited while her sisters entered first. "At least I won't have to worry about those idiots ruining my fences with their everlasting brandy smuggling.

Did you get a chance to deliver my warning, Thomas?"

"Yes, Miss Callie. They was at the inn last night, but they swears they never done it. They say they go through the orchard further down because it's easier ground for the donkeys."

"Ha!" Callie snapped. "I hardly expected them to admit it."

"And," Thomas continued doggedly, "they done gave me a jug of their best brandy for Sir Jason when I told 'em he'd been took sick."

"Hmm," Callie murmured. "That was nice of them, no matter what their motives were. Papa enjoys his after-dinner brandy so. But don't give it to him until I have a chance to ask Dr. Adams if it's all right for him to drink it."

"Yes, Miss Callie." Thomas helped her up into the landaulet and lifted the steps, then closed the door.

Callie subsided back against the worn leather squabs as they began to move. Now that the time to put their plan into action had finally arrived, she felt faint with nervousness. So much depended upon their success. It just had to work. It had to. She repeated the words as if the very force of her desires could make it come true.

The lights of Applewood, the squire's home, shown welcomingly through the long front windows as Thomas pulled the old landaulet up to the door. It opened to reveal Johnston, who favored the three girls with a paternal smile. Taking their shawls, he immediately handed them to the footman hovering in the background.

"The guests are assembled in the main salon, if you'll just follow me."

"Take us to them," Callie quipped, trying to lighten the tension she could sense building in Diana.

"Don't worry, Diana," she whispered as the three of them followed behind Johnston. "Men like helpless females."

Diana had time only to give Callie a sick-looking smile before they reached the main salon and were confronted by what seemed like hordes of noisy people.

"Miss Sutcliff, Miss Olivia, and Miss Diana." Johnston's sonorous tones dropped into the silence that fell as the assembled company caught sight of the beautiful Diana.

"Welcome, welcome, my dears." Ada bustled over and, under cover of the hug she gave Callie, managed to whisper to her, "Congratulations, Diana looks positively delightful. The earl's attention was riveted when he caught sight of her.

"You must meet everyone," Ada continued in a louder voice, guiding the newcomers further into the room. "Of course you already know Emmet Hadley." Ada stopped by the tall young man standing by himself beside the blazing fire.

"Good evening." Emmet addressed Callie, while managing to avoid looking at Olivia. "As you can see, Callie, I've given up being a recluse."

"So I see," Callie murmured inanely, thrown off balance by Emmet's being there. She certainly didn't need any added complications in the form of Olivia's lost love. One quick look at Olivia's pinched white face tore at Callie's heart, and she almost sighed with relief as Ada moved on to the next group.

"Monsieur d'Armagnac, one of our French allies." Ada introduced a stockily built young man dressed to dandified perfection in skin-tight beige pantaloons, a coat of blue bath superfine with huge silver buttons, and an elaborately tied neckcloth that kept his chin permanently elevated.

"Enchanté, mesdemoiselles," he greeted all three, but his gaze lingered on Diana's golden beauty.

"Tristam." Ada dismissed her brother-in-law and Callie was surprised at how much he had seemed to have aged. Although he had been home before, this was the first time she had seen him in eighteen months, and the change was remarkable. He looked ten years older. Tristam Varden had been sampling the free-and-easy life of London a little too liberally, Callie thought with a flash of unease as she remembered Ada's various references to Tristam's gambling debts.

"Mr. and Mrs. Charles Parr." Ada nodded to the couple sitting on a delicate giltwood sofa. The bulky old man lurched to his feet, managed to mutter a "charmed," and then limply flowed back down.

A sot, Callie concurred with Ada's original estimation and then turned to his wife, her eyes widening slightly at the woman's sultry beauty. Mrs. Parr's glossy black hair was arranged in an elaborate Grecian knot with several curls left free to caress her milk-white skin. Huge brown eyes were set in the classic perfection of her face, and her scarlet dress was cut so deeply in the bodice that Callie found herself blushing as she contemplated what would happen if Mrs. Parr should sneeze.

"Mrs. Sutcliff, isn't it?" Mrs. Parr grinned maliciously up at Callie, giving Callie no doubt that the woman was being deliberately obtuse. "You have such lovely daughters."

The viciousness of the attack struck Callie as ridiculous, and her clear laughter rang out with unmistakable amusement.

"Despite the fact that I quite often feel old enough to be their mother, Mrs. Parr, I'm afraid I can't claim the privilege. I'm merely their older sister. I imagine they do seem very young, though, to someone of your age." Callie delivered the thrust with a gentle smile and ignored the choked laugh that Emmet hastily turned into a cough.

"And this—" Ada was almost indecent in her haste to remove Callie from Mrs. Parr's vicinity—"is the Earl of Rutledge and his ward, James Kershaw, who is still feeling a bit pulled."

Taking a deep breath, Callie risked a hasty glimpse up and found herself looking straight into the stranger's black eyes.

"M-my lord," Callie murmured.

"Miss Sutcliff." Rutledge bowed, his face showing nothing more than polite acknowledgment. There was no flash of recognition in his gleaming eyes.

Perhaps he didn't recognize her. She hugged the faint hope to her as she moved to shake James Kershaw's hand, her mind barely registering the slight young man.

Covertly, Callie watched the earl's face as Diana was introduced to him, but his social mask remained firmly in place, and Callie wasn't able to hazard a guess as to his reaction to Diana's physical perfection.

"Callie," Ada began, only to be interrupted by Johnston with the intelligence that the nursery maid wanted to see her. "Humdudgeon!" Ada grimaced. "That girl is afraid to turn around without asking first."

"I'll go see what she wants," Callie offered, only too eager to remove herself from Rutledge's vicinity.

"Oh, would you, Callie?" Ada breathed thankfully. "I hate to leave my guests."

"It will be a pleasure," Callie assured her with perfect truth, and hurried up to the nursery on the third floor. As Ada had suspected, it took only a matter of minutes to deal with the nursemaid's trivial problem. Callie was walking down the hallway on the second floor when she heard the sound of a door opening and, to her horror, Rutledge appeared in front of her. Her heart started beating overtime at the sight of him and she took a deep breath to steady her breathing.

"Good evening, my lord," she said, uncertain as to whether she should pretend yesterday hadn't happened or apologize for it.

His reponse left her in no doubt that he recognized her.

"Good evening, Aunt Callie. I trust you haven't come down with an inflammation of the lungs as a result of your half-dressed state yesterday?"

Callie flushed. "I wasn't half-dressed!" she snapped. "I was just . . . just . . ."

"Setting a new fashion?"

"I don't want to talk about it!" Callie insisted. "And what are you doing up here anyway?"

"I forgot something in my room." Rutledge motioned to the closed door behind him.

"What?" Callie looked suspiciously at his empty hands.

"I don't know," he answered reasonably. "I just said I'd forgotten. If I'd remembered it, I wouldn't have forgotten it."

"But . . ." Callie frowned at him as she tried to make sense out of what he'd said.

Rutledge leaned over and traced an idle finger around

her open lips. "Close your mouth, Aunt Callie. You look like a little trout begging to be caught."

Callie jerked back as his moving finger sent strange shivers of pleasure coursing through her. She ignored them resolutely and pressed her lips together. "I do *not* look like a trout," she snapped.

"No," he agreed, "you look like a Methodist. A less-flattering gown would have been hard to find, especially when contrasted with what your sisters are wearing."

Callie ignored the dismay his words caused. Hadn't that been her whole objective? she demanded of herself. To make Diana look all the more ravishing by comparison. It didn't matter what he thought of her. All that mattered was that Rutledge be bowled over by Diana.

"It isn't polite to comment on a lady's gown," Callie said primly.

"But I find it very hard to remain on conventional terms with you when I remember how you looked hanging from that tree with your dress ripped, your unmentionables flapping in the wind, and—"

"Stop it!" Callie broke in desperately. "It was an accident. I told you. Please forget it."

"Since it distresses you so, of course I'll not refer to it again, although I doubt if I can forget it." He grinned at her.

"We'd best return to the parlor." Callie gave up all attempts to convince him that yesterday was an isolated instance in the uneventful tenor of her life. She'd just have to hope that he'd be so bedazzled by Diana's beauty that he'd overlook her hoydenish behavior.

"As you wish, Miss Sutcliff." Rutledge's abrupt change to society manners brought an inexplicable sense of loss to Callie which she refused to acknowledge. She didn't want to be on familiar terms with Rutledge, she told herself. That way lay sure disaster.

Taking the earl's arm, she allowed him to escort her back to the parlor.

"Now," Ada announced within minutes of their return, "if you're all ready, we'll go in to dinner."

Callie automatically accepted Mr. Parr's arm, trying not to breathe too deeply of the mixed aroma of brandy fumes and unwashed body that enveloped him like a cloud. Her stomach lurched protestingly, its already queasy state not helped any by the not altogether unexpected discovery that the stranger was Rutledge. Although she had tried to ignore the possibility, there were just too few strangers in Thornton Dene for him to have been anyone else. But Rutledge hadn't seemed too appalled by her escapade. On the other hand he also hadn't seemed to have been bowled over by Diana, the unwelcome thought intruded. But what had she expected him to do? she asked herself. Clutch his breast and declare undying devotion on the spot? The very thought of the elegant earl behaving in so farouche a fashion caused her lips to twitch, and she was hard pressed to suppress the laughter that threatened to bubble over. Fortunately, Mr. Parr's frequent inroads into the brandy bottle had rendered him totally insensitive to anything as ephemeral as his dinner companion's moods.

Callie sank into her seat at her host's left and surreptitiously studied the seating arrangements. To her relief, Ada had excelled herself. Rutledge was seated on his hostess's right with Diana beside him, while Mrs. Parr had been relegated to a seat at the squire's end of the table, giving Diana a clear field. A field made all the easier by the helpful Ada, who proceeded to ignore the earl, forcing him to give Diana his undivided attention.

At least Diana had mastered the art of blushing, Callie reflected cynically as she glanced at the pair across from her, and was immediately horrified by the cattish thought. Somehow Callie still thought of Rutledge as the stranger, and *her* stranger at that. She didn't want to share him with anyone, but that was a line of reasoning she wasn't willing to explore, and she determinedly turned from the sight of Rutledge's black head bent over Diana's pink-and-white loveliness.

A quick look at Olivia was sufficient to show Callie that her sister was engaged in conversation with d'Armagnac and giving a very good imitation of a lighthearted flirt without a care in the world. Emmet Hadley was sitting directly across the table, glowering at Olivia. Really! Callie glared furiously at him when she managed to catch his eyes. Emmet Hadley was nothing but a dog in the manger. He didn't want Olivia himself, but neither did he want anyone else to have her.

Since Squire Varden was deep in conversation with Mrs. Parr, Callie turned to talk to Tristam, who was seated on her left, but that turned out to be an exercise in futility. Although Tristam managed to rouse himself sufficiently to respond to direct queries, he answered in monosyllables before again lapsing into silence. His behavior was so far removed from the lively, gregarious young man she had known that Callie couldn't help wondering if he hadn't been keeping Mr. Parr company at the brandy bottle, but she could detect no signs of drunkenness. Just total apathy, she decided, interspersed with halfhearted attempts to respond to the social situation in which he found himself.

Finally, Callie gave up all pretense of being the polite guest and fell into a sleepy silence, making no attempt to force down any of the interminable courses.

After what seemed like years to Callie's numbed senses, Ada finally stood and gave the signal for the ladies to withdraw, leaving the men to their port.

"Now don't be long," Ada admonished her husband, who tore his glazed eyes away from Mrs. Parr's décolletage long enough to mumble something which satisfied his wife.

Callie slipped out of her chair without waiting to see whether Tristam would manage to rouse himself sufficiently to help her.

"What do you think?" Ada hissed, pulling Callie back slightly to let the other women make their way to the main salon.

"Why ask me? You were the one sitting beside them. What do you think?" Callie countered.

"He was certainly attentive," Ada admitted, "but that could simply have been good manners coming to the fore. The way I ignored him, he didn't have any choice but to devote himself to her."

Callie suppressed an impulse to tell Ada a few home truths about her precious earl's vaunted manners and instead asked, "Do you think he's smitten?"

"I don't see how he could help but be," Ada proclaimed loyally and then burst into giggles. "This must have been the strangest dinner party I've ever given. What with my ignoring the guest of honor, Mr. Parr falling asleep over the vegetables, and Mrs. Parr trying out her wiles on Gervais. The poor darling!" Ada giggled again. "He didn't have the foggiest notion what had hit him. And then Emmet glaring across the table as if he was understudying Macbeth."

"Hamlet," Callie corrected her. "Hamlet brooded, Macbeth killed."

"Emmet certainly looked mad enough to kill someone. Are you sure he isn't interested in Olivia?"

"Positive!" Callie said shortly. "And don't you dare try your hand at matchmaking. Olivia would never forgive us."

"I wouldn't dream of it," Ada protested. "Besides, we'll be so busy attaching the earl that we won't have time to worry about Olivia. Maybe she can amuse herself with his ward. Mr. Kershaw is too young for her, but he's a sweet lad."

"Hmm, perhaps," Callie murmured. "Dearest Ada, after the men join us, would you ask me to sing and then ask Diana?"

"Sing!" Ada stared at Callie as if she'd lost her mind. "But, Callie, you can't sing a note. At least, not in tune."

It was a time-honored family joke that it had taken Providence four tries before it had managed to create a truly fine singer. For Callie, the oldest, couldn't carry a tune in a bucket; Olivia had a faint voice; Diana a sweet one, although it lacked true range and depth; while Rosalind had the voice of an angel.

"That's the whole idea," Callie explained. "After I mutilate a song, Diana will sound superb in comparison."

"You don't mind?" Ada eyed her doubtfully.

"I can't say that I exactly relish making a cake of myself, but it's in a good cause. Just remember to ask Diana immediately after me or the impact will be lost."

"If you say so." Clearly Ada had her doubts. "We'd best go. The others will be wondering what happened to us."

The men apparently took to heart Ada's directive not to linger because they appeared a short time later without the drunken Mr. Parr.

"Mr. Parr was indisposed," Gervais told his wife. "His valet saw him straight to bed."

"Poor man." Ada accepted the lie with equanimity and then waited while the men found themselves seats.

Callie breathed a sigh of relief when Rutledge, with his pale ward in attendance, found himself a seat on the sofa which held Diana and herself. She scooted a little closer to Diana to allow James Kershaw to be seated, too.

"Callie," Ada requested when everyone was settled, "please give us the pleasure of your singing."

Emmet's gasp of protest was clearly audible in the silence which greeted Ada's words.

"Oh but, Ada, don't you remember—" Olivia began, only to be interrupted by Callie's bright "I'd love to, Ada. It's always a pleasure to oblige."

Callie walked over to the spinet and exhaled deeply. Turning to face the company, she clasped her hands together, fixed her eyes on a dismal-looking portrait of one of the squire's early ancestors, and began to sing an Italian aria. The only aspect of the song its author would have recognized were the words. The melody—or lack of it—was entirely Callie's own. She stole a quick glance at her audience and, emboldened by their glassy-eyed stares, purposefully exaggerated it.

There was an infinitesimal pause as she finished, as if her audience were trying to decide between honesty and politeness. Politeness prevailed and there was a short smattering of applause. Pleased with the success of her stratagem, Callie moved to sit down, only to be halted by Rutledge's voice.

"Allow me to congratulate you on your rendition of that song, Miss Sutcliff. I've never heard anyone quite in your class before," the bland voice continued. "Would you please favor us with a second selection?"

"Another song?" Callie's mouth fell open and she stared at him in suspicion. The man was tone-deaf or hatefully sarcastic, and it was impossible to tell which by looking into his politely smiling face.

"I'd love to." Callie tossed her head, determined to see it through to the bitter end.

Mercifully, for all concerned, the second song Callie chose was a short lullaby.

"How delightful." Ada roused herself to her duty as hostess, as Callie hurriedly resumed her seat. "Diana, would you—"

"Oh, no," Rutledge interrupted her, "a performance like Miss Sutcliff's couldn't possibly be equaled, and it would be unfair to poor Miss Diana to ask her to try." He smiled gently at the nervous Diana.

"But I'm sure—" Callie began, only to find herself ignored.

"Perhaps we could have a rubber or two of whist?" Rutledge went on to suggest.

"Only if I can be your partner." Mrs. Parr's smile at the earl was an open invitation.

"What a charming prospect," Rutledge agreed. "Squire?" He turned to Gervais Varden.

"Yes? I'm sorry, my lord, I was..."

"Still lost in admiration for Miss Sutcliff's singing?" Rutledge suggested.

"Um, yes." The Squire turned red and then eagerly opted for a game of whist.

The sarcastic beast. Callie shot Rutledge a furious glare which was met by a look of such puzzled bewilderment that for a moment Callie was deceived, until she saw the twinkle in the depths of his ebony eyes.

"Come, Theron dear." Mrs. Parr slipped her arm through Rutledge's and rubbed her body up against him. For all the world like a barn cat, Callie thought, wrinkling her nose in fastidious distaste and turning away. But not before she caught the deepening of the twinkle in Rutledge's eyes.

The game of whist was quickly organized with Rutledge

and Mrs. Parr playing against Tristam and the squire. Much to Callie's surprise, Emmet pulled up a chair and proceeded to watch the game with determined joviality. It was almost as if he were setting out to prove to whoever was interested that losing an arm hadn't affected him in the slightest.

A quick glance at Diana showed Callie that Rutledge's ward was still on the sofa beside her and was trying his best to be entertaining. A good thing, too, and Callie gave the young man an encouraging smile. Not only would it be good for Diana to be on terms with Rutledge's family, but James Kershaw's attentions would divert Diana's thoughts from the brazen way that Mrs. Parr was throwing herself at the earl's head.

"Sit down and talk to me." Ada interrupted Callie's perusal of the room and motioned her into a seat.

"But Olivia . . ." Callie looked around for her other sister.

"Livy's over at the spinet, flirting with d'Armagnac."

Callie sighed for Olivia's obvious unhappiness and turned to Ada. "First, tell me what Emmet's doing here. This is the first time he's been to a social event since he came home."

"I know." Ada nodded. "That's why, when he asked if he could come to dinner tonight, I said yes, despite the fact that it made the numbers uneven."

"He asked you!"

"As good as. I was surprised, too. He came by this afternoon for tea, and, when I mentioned the party tonight, he said it sounded like fun, and now that he was feeling better he'd have to get out more. What else could I do but invite him?"

"How subtle." Callie smiled.

"Emmet Hadley hasn't a subtle bone in his body!"

"That's true," Callie responded thoughtfully, gazing at the young man in question. "I'd almost forgotten what he used to be like."

"I'm going to sneak up and check on Mary." Ada glanced at the card players. "Her teeth are bothering her again, poor lamb."

"I'll keep Miss Sutcliff company while you're gone." Rutledge's voice from right behind Callie caused both women to jump.

"Certainly, my lord." Preoccupied with her daughter, Ada missed the plea in Callie's eyes and hurried off.

"I thought you were playing whist, my lord." Callie glanced over to the card table only to encounter a petulant look from Mrs. Parr's magnificent brown eyes.

"I am." Rutledge sat down beside her. "But at the moment I'm the dummy."

Callie pressed her lips together and refused to take advantage of the opening he'd given her, but the gleam in her eye gave her away.

"Such restraint, Aunt Callie," Rutledge mocked.

"I don't know what you mean." Callie frowned at him and then decided to use the unexpected opportunity to press Diana's suit. "My sister Diana is certainly in looks tonight." Callie nodded toward the couch where Diana was deep in conversation with James Kershaw.

"A lovely child," Rutledge agreed carelessly.

"She isn't a child!" Callie protested. "She's all of eighteen."

"A great age." Rutledge's black eyes twinkled at her. "Especially when viewed from your advanced years. You never did tell me why you are wearing that apology for a dress."

"Because I'd look excessively silly sitting here without it!" Callie fired back, incensed that he should comment again on her unbecoming gown.

"Oh, I wouldn't say that," Rutledge drawled as his slow gaze roamed over her figure, lingering on her firm, high breasts which not even the shapeless bodice could entirely hide. "Provocative, perhaps; exciting, definitely, but never silly."

Callie felt a swell of fascination surge through her at his outrageous words. A fascination she felt honor bound to deny. "You shouldn't speak to me like that. And what's more, what I wear is my own concern."

"Theron, darling, do come along," Mrs. Parr called across

the room. "We're dealing out a new hand."

"Duty calls, Aunt Callie." Rutledge smiled at her. "And just when the conversation was getting interesting."

"You mean indecent," Callie retorted.

"Nonsense. But if you really want an indecent conversation, Aunt Callie, remind me the next time we meet, and I'll do my best to oblige."

Callie refused to rise to his taunt, contenting herself with an expressive sniff as he moved back to Mrs. Parr and the whist game.

- 5 -

CALLIE SLIPPED OUT of her father's bedroom and quietly closed the door, shaking her head at Rosalind when she started to say something. Motioning toward the front stairs, Callie took her sister's arm.

"But I wanted to see Papa," Rosalind said the moment they reached the entrance hall. "It's my turn to sit with him."

"I know." Callie smiled at her. "He mentioned how much he was looking forward to your reading to him, but he fell asleep, and it's much better to let him rest."

"That's true," Rosalind responded, mollified by the mention of the pleasure that her reading program was going to bring. "I can read to him this afternoon when he wakes up."

"Is luncheon ready yet?"

"We've already eaten. We'd have waited for you, but we didn't know how long you'd be. Besides, I was starving," Rosalind added ingenuously.

"So am I. I hope you left me something to eat."

"Yes, plenty. Olivia wasn't hungry and Diana spent the

whole time staring off into space and sighing. If that's what getting married does to you, I'm going to be an old maid like you, Callie."

"How nice," Callie said dryly, trying to ignore the desolate feeling caused by Rosalind's words. It was marvelous that Diana had succumbed to Rutledge's undoubted charms, she tried to tell herself. It would be far better for Diana if she were in love with her husband.

"When's the wedding?" Rosalind asked.

"What? What wedding?"

"Diana and the earl's," Rosalind explained patiently.

"Don't rush your fences. He just met her last night. These things take time."

"Not always," Rosalind insisted. "In *Isabella's Quest*, the duke was so overcome by Isabella that he paid his addresses the very next morning."

"Well, since it's past one, I think it's safe to assume that this earl isn't similarly inclined. Besides, Rosalind," Callie continued, entering the dining room, "it has to be a lot harder when you're dealing with a real person than a fictional character you can manipulate."

"What is?" Olivia looked up from the cup of tea she was drinking.

"Bringing Rutledge up to scratch." Callie pulled out a chair and sat down. "No one could be caught as easily as Isabella's duke."

"I'll get your luncheon, Callie," Rosalind offered. "Cook put it in the kitchen ovens so it would stay warm."

"Thank you, dear." Callie watched Rosalind leave, her limp more pronounced than usual, then frowned and turned to Olivia. "Did Rosalind say anything about her foot? She seems to be dragging it worse than usual."

"It's the cold, I think." For a brief moment, Olivia shared her sister's concern. "The temperature dropped last night. I had ice crystals in my water pitcher this morning."

"We'll have to keep her occupied with reading to Papa. His room is the warmest in the house."

"Here you are." Rosalind made her careful way back

into the room, the tray balanced precariously on her weak arm.

Callie ignored the impulse to grab the tray before something happened, knowing from experience that Rosalind hated to have attention drawn to her disability.

"Thank you, dear." Callie breathed an inward sigh of relief as the tray reached the table in one piece. "Rosalind, please find Diana and tell her that we're leaving for the village just as soon as I finish eating. Then find Nanny and ask her whether she wants me to bring anything back for her."

"Diana's in the morning room, contemplating her projected state of connubial bliss," Olivia sneered.

"What?" Rosalind looked blankly at Olivia.

"Olivia means that Diana is thinking about how nice it will be to be married," Callie translated.

"Then why didn't she say so!" Rosalind sniffed and left the room.

"A good question." Callie eyed Olivia with misgivings. Surely Olivia didn't intend to treat them to a repeat performance of last night's mood.

"I'm sorry." Olivia's lips twisted into a wry grimace. "I guess that Diana's blissful state just grates. I think I'm simply jealous!" Olivia related in a burst of candor.

"But connubial bliss?" Callie questioned, deliberately trying to keep the conversation light.

"I read it in a book once," Olivia giggled, "and I always liked the sound of it. It rather rolls off your tongue."

"Is Diana really all that blissful over the earl?" Callie asked curiously.

"Someone definitely set her all aflutter. She's been mooning around like a sick calf, talking about June weddings and the like."

"Hmmm." Callie concentrated on feeling glad for her sister. "That's half the battle won. Now all we have to do is bring the earl to a similar frame of mind."

"I don't know, Callie." Olivia nibbled thoughtfully on her lower lip. "I get the distinct feeling that underneath that polite exterior of his he's laughing at us."

"Oh?" Callie looked up from the roll she was buttering. "Why's that?"

"Dash it, Callie, it isn't like you to be so thick-headed. Look at the way he asked you to sing a second song. And did you notice how he hung all over Mrs. Parr?"

"How Mrs. Parr hung all over him," Callie corrected her. "And what should he have done about it anyway? He's a guest in Ada's house. He can hardly cause a scene."

"If you ask me, he didn't want to!" Olivia snapped.

"Probably not," Callie admitted honestly. "I can't really see many men turning down what she was offering. But there's a world of difference between a casual affair and marriage. I'd be willing to bet my last shilling that the earl wouldn't marry her even if he could."

"Oh, I don't know," Olivia began.

"It's only common sense, Livy," Callie insisted. "He's a proud man and if Mrs. Parr is willing to have an affair with him, she'd do it with someone else, too. He wouldn't risk that kind of scandal attached to his name. No, he may bed the Mrs. Parrs of the world, but when he marries it'll be to a woman of spotless reputation."

"But who wants a husband who has affairs?"

"Nothing in this world is perfect, Livy, and if there were any alternative, I'd take it. But what can I do? We have to find a husband, and the earl is our only prospect. Besides, according to Ada, having a mistress is the accepted thing among the *haut ton*."

"I guess so, and, if Diana doesn't mind, why should we?"

"I'm taking Diana into the village. Would you like to come too, Livy?"

"No." Olivia shook her head. "It's too cold out there and, anyway, I don't want to run into that rake."

"What rake?" Callie looked startled.

"Emmet Hadley!" Olivia snapped. "Did you ever see anything like him last night! Glaring at me all through dinner, and then ignoring me afterward just to watch them play whist!"

"Well . . ." Callie tried to think of some comforting comment, but none came to mind.

"I'll show him, though." Olivia tossed her head. "He didn't like it one little bit when I flirted with the Frenchman. He wants me to sit home and wear the willow for him while he has his Spanish lady, but I'm going to flirt with d'Armagnac every chance I get!" Olivia dropped her cup and rushed from the room.

Callie sighed, wishing with all her heart that there was something she could do to help Olivia, but there wasn't. Olivia would have to solve her problem by herself. Callie hoped only that she didn't do anything too outrageous in the process and embroil them all in scandal broth.

Rosalind limped back into the room. "Nanny says would you please stop at the greengrocer's for some lemons. The big yellow ones, not some that he's had for weeks. Then pick up some calves'-foot jelly from the chemist's, and a nice piece of whitefish from the fishmonger's to poach for Papa's dinner."

"Fine. Tell her I'll demand to see all of Mr. Jones's lemons before I make a choice." Callie laughed. Despite having dealt with the local merchants for the past thirty-five years, Nanny still firmly believed that they were waiting only for a lapse in her eternal vigilance before they robbed her blind. "Did you find Diana?"

Rosalind nodded. "She was in the morning room, sitting at the window staring outside."

"Did you tell her that I wanted her?" Callie asked impatiently.

"Yes, she did," Diana herself answered as she came into the room, "but, if it's all the same to you, Callie, I'd rather stay home. Someone might come to call."

"No, it's not all the same to me." Callie tried to keep the exasperation she was feeling out of her voice. "We have to order some new gowns for you, and I can't do that if you're not there."

"New gowns?" Diana's face lit up, and it was obvious that she was sorely tempted.

"Several," Callie added, sweetening the bait. "Ada's

holding some parties to help us and you'll need new clothes for them."

"What kind of parties?" Diana asked.

"Two balls, although one is a masquerade. You have to come as your grandmother."

"Poor men!" Diana giggled.

"Or grandfather, as the case may be," Callie continued, unperturbed. "That's to be this Saturday, and then later she's having a real ball. It'll be lovely."

"Yes," Diana breathed, a faraway look in her eyes. "I'll wear a white silk gown with tiny glittering diamonds that'll sparkle like the stars in the candlelight as I come floating down the staircase. Rowena wore a dress like that in a book called *Rowena's Reward.*"

"Well," Callie temporized, "we can't afford diamonds— even tiny ones—and you can't very well come down the staircase because it isn't our house. You'll have to come in through the front door like everyone else."

"I suppose." Diana acknowledged the truth of what Callie was saying. "But I can still make an entrance."

"Of course you can," Callie consoled her. "But for now, run and get your pelisse and you'd best bring gloves and a hood. It's freezing outside."

"I won't be a minute." Diana all but ran from the room.

At least one of them was happy. Callie sighed and pushed back her chair.

They reached the village thirty frozen minutes later and drove straight to the inn, where they left Nebuchadnezzar in the charge of the ostler.

They were able to find several dress lengths for Diana, a fact which pleased Callie no end. Not so pleasing was the information the store's proprietress imparted.

"Have you seen those guests of the squire's yet?" Without waiting for an answer she rushed on. "That Mrs. Parr was in the village yesterday afternoon with that earl and a proper hussy she was, too, a-hanging on his arm an' a-whispering in his ear. And her with a husband of her own back at the squire's!" The woman was outraged.

"They were in the village yesterday afternoon?" Callie

tried to tell herself that the dismay she felt was due solely to concern for Diana's tender sensibilities.

"Oh, he doesn't like her," Diana announced, shrugging off Mrs. Parr. "He just doesn't want to be rude to her while he's a guest at the squire's. Mr. Kershaw said so."

"Oh," Callie murmured as the implications of what Diana had said struck her. Rutledge must indeed be interested in Diana if he'd instructed his ward to reassure her about Mrs. Parr. But, strangely enough, the fact brought her no joy and it required a real effort to convince herself that she was pleased with the first signs of success of their plans.

An hour later they had completed their shopping and were headed back toward the inn and the promise of tea.

"Would you like me to carry the fish, Callie?" Diana asked.

"No, it's no problem. It's not heavy, just awkward, and you've got the calves'-foot jelly. We can't risk dropping it because it might break. Brrr." Callie lowered her head into the icy wind. "Let's hurry. I can't wait to get my tea."

The walk to the inn took less than ten minutes. They hurried up the well-swept wooden steps and in through the stout oak door.

"What might I do for you, Miss Callie?" The innkeeper hurried over to them, wiping his wet hands on the dirty linen apron tied around his ample waist.

"Tea, a plate of your delicious cream cakes, and the private parlor, please, Mr. Larkin. I think we're frozen." Callie laughed.

"Well now, Miss Callie." He shifted uncomfortably. "The tea and cream cakes be easy enough, but the parlor's bespoken."

"Bespoken!" Callie sounded as surprised as she was. Thornton Dene was a tiny village well off the main roads. Visitors who would demand a private parlor were rare at any time of year and unheard of in this kind of weather.

"Oh, Callie," Diana moaned. "Can't we just sit down in a corner of the common room? I'm so cold."

Undecidedly, Callie glanced around the crowded room. It looked as if most of the idle fishermen had congregated there, as well as a large segment of the farming community. Much as she wanted to accede to Diana's request, it just wasn't done. Young women of their class simply didn't sit in public rooms, despite the fact that Callie could probably have named everyone in it. The men themselves would have been uncomfortable.

"I'm sorry, Diana," Callie began and then broke off as she caught sight of Abner Varden, with the disreputable George clutched to his chest, leaning up against the wall by the fireplace.

"What on earth!" Callie motioned for Abner to come over, wondering what he was doing there. Ada would be furious.

"Abner, what are you doing here?" She moved slightly out of the landlord's hearing. "Does your Mama know where you are?"

"It's all right. I came with Uncle Tristam," Abner assured her.

"Then where is he?" Callie looked around again. "I don't see him."

"He met some men and they went up there." Abner pointed toward the stairs which led to the second-floor bedrooms. "He said he wouldn't be very long, but he has," Abner complained. "Me and George is starved. Look at him." Abner held the beast out toward Callie so that she could properly appreciate the cat's emaciated state. This maneuver proved to be a definite mistake because George, catching the scent of the fish Callie was carrying, decided to take the problem of adequate nourishment into his own paws. Emitting an earsplitting howl, he launched himself at Callie, his sharp claws digging red furrows across her hand.

Startled, Callie jerked back, sending the lemons flying in all directions while George held on to the leaking fish package for dear life.

After a moment of stunned silence, Diana screamed at the sight of the blood on Callie's hand and began sobbing at the top of her lungs.

"Be quiet, Diana!" Callie snapped, shaking the package

of fish in a vain attempt to dislodge George.

"Don't hurt him, Aunt Callie!" Abner shrieked, fearful for his pet.

"I'm the one who's bleeding, Abner! Diana, do control yourself!" Callie swung around to comfort her sister, stepped on a loose lemon, and fell backward, her head slamming against the heavy maple table. For a brief moment the cacophony of sound sharpened before it abruptly ceased, and she slipped into merciful oblivion, still holding on to her father's dinner like grim death.

"Aunt Callie, Aunt Callie." The insistent voice slithered through the fog covering her numbed mind and she tried to respond, but without any success.

Strong, gentle fingers stroked her hair back from her hot forehead and then trailed lightly down her cheek, leaving sensual shivers of awareness in their wake.

"Hmmm," Callie murmured at the delightful sensations and then nuzzled her face against the hard palm of the caressing hand.

"Come on, Aunt Callie, open your eyes and look at me."

The worried voice interrupted her lips's exploration and she muttered a protest. She didn't want to wake up. She wanted to continue to bask in the feel of the hard fingers on her sensitive skin.

"Aunt Callie!" The imperious voice wouldn't be denied, and she opened her eyes reluctantly.

Rutledge's broad shoulders filled her vision and she smiled dreamily at the massive body bent over her. Her eyes fastened on his firm mouth, and her small pink tongue licked her dry lips in an unconsciously provocative gesture. Curiosity about what it would feel like if Rutledge pressed those firm lips against her soft ones, if his hands began to caress more than just her flushed cheeks, flitted through her muddled mind.

She raised her hand bemusedly and gently touched his face, tracing the line of his lips with her exploring finger. Her gaze shifted and collided with his. The tiny reddish glow in the back of his ebony eyes finally penetrated Callie's pain-induced lethargy, and she blinked in horror as she realized exactly what she had been doing. Whatever must he think of her wanton behavior? Probably very little, Callie realized with painful honesty. She was neither pretty enough nor feminine enough to appeal to his senses, and he was much too honest to pretend, she admitted regretfully. She winced at the direction of her thoughts, angry at her own lack of pride. The anger gave her the courage to address him.

"Good afternoon, my lord," she said, deeming this one of those times when the less said, the better.

"Good afternoon, Aunt Callie." He disappeared from her line of vision for a moment and then returned, holding a thick brown mug. He leaned over her, slipped an arm under her shoulders, and pulled her up against his hard chest. "Drink this down," he ordered.

Resolutely, Callie tried to shut out the feel of her body crushed up against his and to concentrate on more mundane matters. "What is it?" she asked, only to have him take advantage of her open mouth and tip a good portion of the mug's contents down her throat. "Augh!" she shuddered when he was finally satisfied and lowered her back down on the horsehair sofa. "That was awful! What was it?"

"Brandy, my dear." He finished the contents of the mug and set it down. "Superb brandy, as a matter of fact. I'm not sure I've ever had its equal, and certainly not in some tiny village in the middle of nowhere."

"If that's good brandy, then heaven preserve me from bad." Callie lifted a trembling hand and grimaced as she noticed the dried blood on the back of it. "What happened?" She looked vaguely around the room, which she immediately recognized as the inn's only private parlor.

"As near as I could make sense of the various garbled versions, you fought George for the fish and lost. When I came out, you were lying on the floor, dead to the world, your sister was having strong hysterics, and George was eating the fish."

Callie looked up into Rutledge's calm face and felt laughter bubbling up. She pressed her lips together, desperately trying to suppress it, but it escaped all the same. "I'm sorry," she gasped, "but it's so ridiculous. That cat will be the death of me yet."

"He's making progress." Rutledge didn't seem to share her humor at the situation. "Your head took a nasty crack. You've been unconscious for the past ten minutes."

"I wish I still were." Callie moaned. "My head aches."

"It's no wonder," Rutledge snapped. "Heads weren't made to be used as battering rams."

"Now see here," Callie began indignantly, only to be interrupted by a knock on the door.

"Come in," Rutledge called.

The door opened to admit the landlord, who was carrying a tray that held a steaming pot of tea, a bowl of warm water, a towel, and several jars.

"Oh, Miss Callie." The innkeeper looked pale as he anxiously studied her face. "I was so worried. I thought you were dead when you just lay there all still like a corpse."

"As you can see, she isn't." Rutledge held the door in a silent invitation for the innkeeper to leave. "Apart from a nasty headache and a few scratches, she's in excellent shape."

"Yes, m'lord." The innkeeper left, obviously more than a little overawed by the earl.

"I think we'd best dress those scratches first. Sit up, Aunt Callie." He put an arm under her shoulders and pulled her up.

"You don't have to," Callie mumbled. "Diana will..." It struck her suddenly that Diana wasn't there. "Where's Diana?" She tried to get to her feet, but the room swayed alarmingly, and she felt herself enfolded in Rutledge's strong arms.

"Sit still, Aunt Callie." He pushed her back onto the hard sofa.

"But Diana!" she protested. "She can't stay in the common room by herself, and what are we doing in the private parlor? Mr. Larkin said it was engaged."

"And so it was. By me. But I'm quite willing to share it with you. And do stop worrying about Diana. I had enough to manage, with you unconscious, so I had James drive her home in your pony trap. I'll pick him up when I take you back."

"Diana just went off and left me!" Callie said in disbelief. "Dead, for all she knew!"

"She left because I told her to."

"And people always jump to do your bidding!" Callie snapped.

"Mostly." He smiled at her. "You must admit, my dear Aunt Callie, that the bird-witted Diana is hardly a match for me in a battle of wills."

"She isn't bird-witted," Callie insisted, and then colored under his unwavering stare. "Well, only sometimes."

"A pretty widgeon," Rutledge repeated, "not that that's such a bad thing. She's a very restful person to have around. Especially after an encounter with you."

"That's not fair," Callie argued. "You can hardly blame me because I was attacked by Abner's cat. Good Lord— Abner! I forgot all about him. He can't stay out there. Ada will be furious if she ever finds out. That fribble Tristam probably brought Abner along so that Ada and the squire wouldn't realize he was coming to the inn."

"Really?" Rutledge responded absently, as he took her scratched hand and pushed it gently into the bowl of warm water.

Callie winced, the pain momentarily dulling her indignation at Tristam's irresponsibility.

Rutledge picked up one of the soft linen squares and began carefully bathing away the dried blood. "Why should he want to keep a visit to the village's only inn a secret? Is it Thornton Dene's den of iniquity?"

"No." Callie chuckled at the thought of the innkeeper, who was an elder in the church and a veritable pillar of the community, being involved in anything clandestine. "We haven't got a den of iniquity in Thornton Dene." Callie sighed regretfully. "The only excitement we've had in years was when the baker's wife ran away to America with our last vicar. And you'd have thought they'd have had more consideration, too."

"Certainly." Rutledge lifted her hand out of the brown

stained water and began to pat it dry gently. "A man of the cloth and all that."

"Oh, that wasn't the problem. What made it so bad was the replacement the bishop sent. He's awful." Callie forgot who she was talking to as her indignation got the better of her. "Why, right after Papa's seizure, he came to the house and practically proposed to me."

"And that makes him awful?" Rutledge sounded amused.

"Of course not, but he didn't want to marry me, he wanted the estate and he thought I'd inherit it because I'm the oldest. Once he found out that The Meadings is entailed to my cousin Gilmer, and I won't get a shilling . . ." Callie broke off in horror as she realized what she'd almost blurted out. "I mean," she stammered and then gasped as the ointment he was spreading seemed to burn through her hand.

"Sorry, my dear, but this is necessary. God only knows where that beast has been." He picked up a strip of soft linen and began winding it around her hand. "Perhaps your vicar will improve in time. I would imagine that a small community like this isn't used to strangers."

"No," Callie agreed. "The only strangers we ever see are occasional ones in the summer who get lost on their way to Brighton. Why, even our smugglers . . ." She stopped in confusion. It must have been the brandy making her so talkative, she thought. She tried to turn the subject. "Anyway, you're bound to meet him sooner or later because he's going to ask you about a living on your estates."

"Let's hope it's later." Rutledge rinsed off his hands, dried them, and flung the towel down. "Relax a moment while I find young Varden. I'll be back presently."

- *6* -

CALLIE WATCHED THE door close behind him with heartfelt relief. She desparately needed a few minutes alone to regain her composure. Wearily, she rubbed her aching forehead with her unbandaged hand and leaned back against the hard sofa. It was absolutely uncanny the way Rutledge always managed to catch her at a disadvantage, and all because of that deuced cat, she thought with a flash of asperity. She should have left him up the tree in the first place; then none of this would have happened. Rutledge must be having serious doubts about Diana's family, and it was impossible to tell just how firmly his interest was caught. He'd called Diana a bird-witted female, but on the other hand his tone of voice had been affectionate. And he'd said she was restful, Callie reminded herself, forgetting conveniently the rest of what he'd said. But just what it all added up to, Callie didn't know, and her head ached too much for her to continue to worry the subject.

Leaning forward, she poured out a cup of tea clumsily with her left hand, added cream and sugar, then stirred it.

Burying her nose in the steam, Callie inhaled deeply of the fragrant brew, sipping it eagerly. She looked up as Rutledge came in.

"Did you find him?" she demanded, trying to look behind him to see if Abner was following.

"No." Rutledge shut the door and walked over to the sofa. "The landlord said that Tristam collected Abner and George right after I carried you in here. Presumably he took them home, because they aren't anywhere in the inn."

Rutledge reached down and put a finger under her chin, tilting her head up. He studied her face meticulously. "You're beginning to get some of your natural color back."

"Thank you," Callie mumbled, hoping he hadn't noticed the way her heart had started to pound at his casual touch.

"You're welcome, my dear." Rutledge smiled and poured himself a cup of tea. He sat down beside her on the sofa and began to sip his drink.

Callie shifted, restless at the feel of his hard thigh next to hers.

"Don't fidget, Aunt Callie."

"Don't call me 'Aunt Callie'!" She glared at him. "I told you before that I wasn't your aunt."

"No," he corrected her, "you *tried* to tell me that you weren't my aunt, but you were having problems with your semantics."

"Don't change the subject!" Callie refused to be diverted. "You must see that you can't call me that."

"Why not?" Rutledge looked perplexed. "Abner does, and he's not your nephew."

"Abner happens to be seven years old and you're not."

"I'm four-and-thirty. Was there anything else about me you wanted to know?" he asked. "It'll save you the trouble of leading up to it if you just ask."

"I wasn't hinting for information! I'm not that interested," Callie lied. "Contrary to your fond imaginings, not everyone is overawed by a mere earl."

"Diana is." Rutledge looked amused. "She positively trembles whenever I come near."

Which could have nothing to do with fear, Callie thought, although she could hardly say so.

"Diana is only eighteen, so naturally she's much more susceptible to people and events."

"And you aren't?" Rutledge studied her with sincere interest.

"My experiences are much broader than Diana's, especially concerning men." Callie's voice was unconsciously bitter as she stared down into her steaming tea.

"Oh?" The humor in Rutledge's voice infuriated her, and she blurted out more than she'd meant to.

"I have been engaged!" she snapped. "I know perfectly well what motivates men—money and beauty. In that order. Oh, they'll fill your ears with all kinds of sweet promises, and they're more than willing to dally in the garden with you. At least until a better-looking prospect comes along."

"No, Callie." Rutledge's voice for once held neither mockery nor laughter. "Not they—*he*. One man. You're much too intelligent to condemn all men simply because one was a scoundrel."

"Perhaps." Callie was honest enough to admit the truth of what he was saying, but her bitterness had been a part of her for so long that she found it impossible to change her mind suddenly.

"Now finish that tea," Rutledge ordered. "I want to be going soon. The sun will be going down, and I don't want to be driving these roads after dark."

"Oh, it's perfectly safe," Callie assured him. "The only people likely to be out are the brandy smugglers, and, if you pretend you don't see them, they'll ignore you." Callie put down her half-full cup on the tray.

"Don't you want any more?" Rutledge looked sharply at her.

"No." Callie's smile wavered. "I have the headache still. I'd just like to go home."

"To go home and to bed," Rutledge corrected.

"I can't. I have to sit with Papa tonight."

"I'm sure the sight of your white, pinched face is exactly

what your father needs to assure him that everything is well. Let that other sister of yours sit with him."

"Olivia?" Callie asked absently.

"Yes, the one who was flirting so determinedly with d'Armagnac. Here, stand up." Rutledge grabbed her elbows and hauled her to her feet, keeping a hand on her as she tried to button up her pelisse.

"Olivia isn't a flirt!" Callie denied, while her fingers fumbled with the buttons, Rutledge's nearness making her strangely inept.

He pushed her hands away impatiently and buttoned it up himself. Then he wrapped the hood around her head and helped her to slip a mitten on her good hand. He left the bandaged hand bare.

"Your mitten won't fit over the bandage. You'd best put that hand inside your coat once we get outside."

"Yes, my lord." Callie stuffed the unused mitten in her reticule and watched while Rutledge slipped on a gray driving coat that had at least six shoulder capes.

"What's wrong, Aunt Callie?" He turned around and caught her staring at him.

"Nothing. I just realized that you must be what Tristam was trying to look like," Callie blurted out and blushed scarlet at how personal the remark was. "I meant . . ."

"Never mind, Aunt Callie." Rutledge traced the flood of color up her cheeks. "That's almost a compliment, so leave well enough alone. Come along." He took her arm and guided her out of the room.

Callie was unable to suppress a blush at the way the noise in the common room died away when she entered it. Keeping her eyes on the floor, she tried to ignore the curious stares she was getting. There was no doubt about it, she thought with rueful resignation. She and her encounter with the cat would be the main topic of conversation at a great many dinner tables tonight.

They had almost reached the safety of the door when, to Callie's dismay, it opened and the vicar swaggered in.

"My dear Miss Callie." He greeted her as if they were lifelong friends. "I hope you're feeling more the thing?" He shot a curious glance at Rutledge, who was standing close behind her. "Now, I won't read you a lecture," he said, wagging a finger at her, "even though you know you deserve one. Ladies should be setting an example."

"Good," Rutledge stated.

"Good?" Marston sounded confused.

"Good that you aren't going to read her a lecture. For a moment I thought she was going to be subjected to a load of sanctimonious twaddle."

Marston flushed uncomfortably and turned to glare at someone over by the fireplace who hadn't been quick enough to suppress his amusement at the earl's words.

"I don't believe I've had the pleasure?" Marston looked questioningly at the earl.

"That's right, you haven't," Rutledge agreed, and, stepping around the vicar, he hustled Callie out through the open door and down to the waiting curricle. Without giving her a chance to climb up, he picked her up and swung her into the seat before he skirted the horses and jumped into the seat beside her. He tossed a coin to the ostler, who was holding the animals' heads, and then loosened the reins on the prancing pair.

"What's so funny?" he asked a giggling Callie.

"The look on the vicar's face." She broke into frank laughter. "I've never heard anything so ruthlessly uncivil in my life. I wish I'd have had the nerve to say it." Her voice became wistful. "But I haven't your way about me."

"And a good thing too, madam. Arrogance in a woman is unforgivable. Women should be sweet and gentle."

"Of all the farradiddle!" Callie was outraged. "Women have better things to do than to sit around acting like some fugitive heroine from a bad melodrama!"

"Like climbing trees and fighting cats for fish?"

"I don't think George is a cat. I think he's the reincarnation of a tiger, and he hasn't adjusted to his present form."

"An intriguing possibility," Rutledge said, chuckling, "but nonetheless something will have to be done about him. Perhaps a word to Mrs. Varden?"

"Don't you dare! Ada would be mortified over the trouble

George has caused, and she'd make Abner put him back in the barn."

"Would that be such a bad thing?"

"Right now it would be. Abner loves that mangy beast."

"How about if we were to get him a more acceptable pet, such as a dog?"

"No." Callie rejected the idea. "Children get very attached to the most unlikely things and there's nothing to do but to wait for the interest to wane. I remember once when Emmet's uncle brought him a pair of white mice back from London. Emmet thought they were the most wondrous creatures the good Lord ever made." Callie smiled in remembrance. "He took those things everywhere with him, including church. One Sunday the vicar decided that Emmet could help with the reading, so Emmet gave the box with the mice in it to Olivia to hold. And, of course, Olivia opened it to see what was inside."

"They escaped?"

"Needless to say." Callie grinned. "They were out in a trice. You never saw such a spectacle. Women screaming and yelling and running for the doors. And the poor vicar just standing there in the pulpit, trying to figure out what he'd said that had caused the riot. It took us forever to find the poor things. All the noise had frightened them out of their wits. They never were too lively after that."

"I shouldn't wonder," Rutledge said dryly. "When was all this?"

"A good fifteen years ago. Livy couldn't have been more than six or seven at the time."

"Emmet?" Rutledge frowned. "Would that be the same young man who was to dinner last night?"

Callie nodded. "Emmet Hadley. He, Ada, and I are all of an age. We used to roam the countryside together, with Livy as our devoted shadow. It's a wonder that the poor child ever lived to grow up when I remember some of the things we used to do to her."

"It sounds as if you had a very happy childhood."

"Yes, we were very lucky." Callie sighed. "But it seems so long ago now. Ada's married with a family of her own, and Emmet's lost an arm in the war." Callie's voice trailed away into silence.

"And you've become the mainstay of your family," Rutledge said.

"Well, someone had to run the estate," Callie insisted, sensing criticism in his remark. "Not everyone has the option of retiring to her couch and practicing to be soft and gentle so that someday a man will condescend to marry her!"

"Don't generalize about something you know nothing about."

"Do so!" Callie insisted childishly before she subsided into offended silence, secretly appalled at how she'd let her tongue run away with her. Why should she care that Rutledge liked weak, clinging women? She should be glad, she tried to convince herself. That way he was much more likely to seriously consider Diana for a wife. But this bit of logic only served to sink her further into a morass of self-pity. To her horror, she felt a tear slip down her cheek. Surreptitiously, she reached up to brush it away.

"Cold, Aunt Callie?" Rutledge glanced at her averted face and swore softly under his breath when he caught sight of her tears.

"No." Callie's voice came out high and squeaky. "I have the headache, that's all."

"Poor girl." His gentle voice made her want to cry all the harder. He halted the horses and reached over to pull her up against his shoulder, cradling her slight body against his. Then, with a twist of his powerful arms, he lifted her across his lap.

Callie's breath caught in her throat at the feel of the hard muscles of his thighs pressed into her soft hips. She licked her dry lips and glanced up at him, only to find her gaze ensnared in the gleaming darkness of his eyes. Mesmerized, Callie watched as those eyes came closer and his lips suddenly closed over hers. She melted into him instinctively and, as he felt her response, he gathered her closer, his arms encircling her back and his hand cupping the side of her breast.

His lips hardened, exerting pressure until her own parted

beneath his silent demand. The earl was quick to take advantage of her concession, and his tongue invaded immediately, exploring the warm sweetness of her mouth with sensual thoroughness.

Callie moaned deep in her throat and pressed closer to him, drinking in his potent masculinity as though she were dying of thirst. There was no thought of Diana and their plans in her mind. Nothing existed beyond the sensual magic of his mouth and the euphoric sense of well-being it engendered. Much too soon for her flaming senses, Rutledge lifted her off his lap and started the patiently waiting horses.

"Don't worry, my dear, it'll all come out fine in the end," he comforted her as if the soul-shattering kiss had never occurred.

And how was she supposed to take that? Callie wondered. Was he just uttering a bromide, or did he realize that she had been trying to matchmake and he was telling her he was agreeable? One thing was certain, even to Callie's muddled mind. There was a lot more to the fashionable earl than she had originally thought. The bored exterior that he seemed to don at will hid a sharp mind that absorbed everything that happened around it.

When they arrived, they found Diana and James Kershaw ensconced on the sofa in the morning room sipping tea.

"Callie!" Diana jumped up and rushed to embrace her sister, almost knocking the dizzy Callie off her feet.

"Easy." Rutledge put a steadying hand at Callie's back. "Your sister would be all the better for going to bed. Her head is still bothering her."

"Poor Callie," Diana sympathized. "I can imagine. You looked so awful lying on the floor like that. Come along. I'll help you into bed."

"James." Rutledge's voice brought the bemused James Kershaw to his feet. "Good afternoon, Miss Diana." He bowed to Diana. "And you, miss." He turned to Callie and his voice sharpened. "See that you get to bed at once."

"Good afternoon, my lord," Callie sniffed haughtily, and then, remembering how kind he'd been, was filled immediately with remorse. "Thank you very much for your help this afternoon."

"My pleasure." He grinned at her before hustling the silent James out.

Fifteen minutes later, Callie was in bed with a hot brick at her feet. Sighing, she snuggled a little deeper into the warm, lavender-scented sheets and closed her eyes, letting exhaustion overtake her.

Callie pushed open the attic door and walked in, her three sisters close behind her. "Brr, it's cold up here." She glanced around the dusty attic.

"And dark." Diana peered fearfully into the shadows cast by the stacks of boxes and trunk.

"Open that window behind you, Diana," Callie said. "I don't want to risk lighting a candle up here, and it can't possibly be any colder than it already is."

"Callie," Olivia called from further down the attic. "Come look. This chest is full of gowns. Lovely ones." She pulled out an armful of watered silk. "See."

Callie shook out the dress and held it up against Olivia. "Perfect. It will fit with very little alteration, and that's a blessing if we're going to have them ready for Ada's ball tomorrow. This blue velvet ought to do very nicely for Diana." Callie picked it up.

"How about this one?" Olivia held up a brilliant orange creation that still boasted a feather boa around the deep neckline.

"Mmmm." Callie studied the flamboyant dress with a great deal of interest.

"I was just bamming." Olivia laughed uncertainly.

"For you, yes, but I think it will do very nicely for me. I always wanted feathers."

"Are you sure, Callie?" Olivia sounded uncertain. "It looks so . . . so . . . ."

"Yes, it does, doesn't it?" Callie chuckled. "But if it was good enough for Grandmother, who am I to cavil?"

"Callie! Livy! Come see what we found!" Rosalind's

excited voice called to them.

"What did you find?" Callie obligingly went over to see.

"Wigs." With all the aplomb of a conjurer, Rosalind produced a monstrous white apparition. "Isn't it fabulous?"

"How in the world did they ever manage to stand the weight of these contraptions?" Olivia poked the offending wig with a disdainful finger.

"What are those things stuck in it?" Diana asked.

"Wax fruit." Callie peered closer. "They're slightly melted. Let's see how one of them looks on you, Diana."

"Not mine." Rosalind hugged her fruited prize close to her bony chest. "She can have one of the others."

"Any one will do." Callie reached down and grabbed the first wig that came to hand and stuffed it on Diana's head. "I just want to see if . . ."

"Callie?" Diana quavered. "This wig feels strange."

"Of course it feels strange. You aren't used to it."

"No, I mean it feels like . . ." Her voice trailed off before her perfect rosebud mouth opened to emit a series of piercing screams.

"Diana!" Callie grabbed her, dumbfounded by the turn of events.

"A mouse!" Diana shrieked a second before the terrified rodent scrambled down Diana's arm and disappeared between the boxes. Callie yanked the wig off Diana's head and flung it back into the trunk.

"Stop it, Diana! It's gone. Stop it!" Callie shook her in an attempt to break through her hysterics.

"It was horrible and slimy." Diana's screams subsided into a series of hiccuping sobs.

"Don't be a perfect block, Diana." Rosalind's voice was scathing. "Mice are warm and furry. Snakes are slimy."

"Snakes!" Diana jerked to attention, her haunted eyes daring glances into the impenetrable gloom.

"Thank you, Rosalind Sutcliff!" Callie snapped at her unrepentant sister.

"Well," Rosalind defended herself, "she'd no call to go on like a martyr over one poor little mouse."

"At least that answered my question about whether or

not to wear the wig." Callie endeavored to keep hidden the quiver of laughter in her voice. "Olivia, would you take Diana to her room and give her a composer. Rosalind, check on Papa and make sure that he didn't hear Diana. If he did, make a joke about it."

"A joke!" Diana pulled herself out of her lethargy to object.

"Papa mustn't be worried no matter what happens," Callie repeated for what she was sure was the hundredth time. "And one tiny mouse does not constitute a catastrophe. I'll take these dresses down to the sewing room, and we can start on them when Diana is feeling more the thing." Callie closed the open window and gathered up the chosen dresses, following her sisters out of the attic.

"Miss Callie." Price's soft voice accosted her on the second floor landing. "There are guests in the morning room."

"Not Cousin Joan?" Callie asked with foreboding.

"No, Miss Callie, it's only Miss Ada and some fancy London gentleman."

"Ada?" Callie frowned. "I wonder what...Oh, here, Price." Callie handed him the bundle of dresses. "Please put those in the sewing room."

"Yes, Miss Callie." Price continued down the hallway, his dignity not the least frayed by the armful of feminine frippery he carried.

Callie hurried down the stairs, curious as to what had brought Ada out and which of her visitors was with her. Certainly not Mr. Parr. She stifled a giggle. No one would ever call him fancy.

"Callie, dear," Ada greeted her the moment she entered the room.

"Whatever brings you out in this weather, Ada?" Callie hugged her friend and then glanced around for the London gentleman. She didn't have to look far. Rutledge was leaning against the fireplace mantel. A silver-buttoned coat of blue superfine emphasized his broad shoulders and seemed to deepen the darkness of his crisp black hair, while fashionable dove-colored pantaloons encased his muscular thighs.

"My lord," Callie greeted him coolly, resolutely ignoring

the way her treacherous body quickened to awareness in his presence.

"Miss Sutcliff." Rutledge bowed politely, as if yesterday had never been, and then spoiled the effect by his next words. "I hear Miss Diana is still out of sorts."

"My lord?" Callie looked perplexed.

"Yes, Callie, whatever is the matter with her? We could hear her screaming at the top of her lungs as we drove up. For a horrible moment I thought that—" she paused—"but Price said your Papa is in prime twig."

"Oh!" Callie bit her lip in exasperation, remembering the open window. "It was really my fault, my lord. I put a mouse on her."

"Callie, you didn't!" Ada giggled. "I've often had the urge to pinch her, but a mouse?"

"I didn't do it on purpose. It was hiding in the wig I put on her, and it ran down her arm. You know what exquisite sensibilities Diana has." Callie glared meaningfully at Ada.

"Oh, yes, quite." Ada belatedly remembered the match she was helping to promote. "But actually I came to invite Rosalind to spend the night tomorrow. She'll enjoy watching the first few dances."

"Thank you, Ada." Callie beamed at her friend. "That's very kind of you, but I still don't understand why you had to come all this way in the cold when a note would have done."

"The earl was going to exercise his horses, and he offered to bring me," Ada explained.

"How nice." Callie smiled at her friend, having no doubt that Ada had seized upon the ride as an excuse to bring Rutledge to The Meadings in the hope of furthering Diana's cause.

"I'll get Diana," Callie began, only to be forestalled by Rutledge.

"I wouldn't dream of expecting Miss Diana to visit when she's just suffered such a shattering blow to her sensibilities."

Callie stared at him suspiciously, unable to tell whether

he was being considerate or merely sarcastic. His face remained a polite social mask.

"Besides," he continued, "it's much too cold to leave the horses standing."

"Of course." Callie swallowed her disappointment at having missed an opportunity to bring Diana to his notice. She glanced at Ada, who grimaced, as if to disclaim all responsibility for the shortness of the visit.

"Thank you again for Rosalind's invitation," Callie told Ada as she hugged her good-bye.

"Good afternoon, Miss Sutcliff." Rutledge bowed over her hand. "I hope Miss Diana recovers from her vapors."

"Yes," Callie answered shortly, certain now that he was mocking her. "I'll tell her that you were asking after her."

"Then you'd best paraphrase what I said," Rutledge added before he escorted Ada out.

- 7 -

"DIANA, IF YOU drop anything, be careful how you bend over to pick it up. Those hoops are a positive menace." Callie pulled Diana's skirt a little more firmly into place over the pannier cage and then backed up to study the effect. "The looped style a la polonaise suits you, and the color makes your eyes bluer."

"They wear hoops at court," Olivia said. "I read about it in the *Ladies Magazine*. The queen doesn't like modern fashions."

"Never mind the queen." Rosalind was almost beside herself with excitement. "Let's hurry. Something might happen, and we'll miss it."

"Nothing will happen," Callie soothed her. "Have you packed a nightgown?"

"And a toothbrush," Rosalind said. "I gave my bag to Price to put in the landaulet so I wouldn't forget it."

"Fine." Callie adjusted the pink velvet bow in Rosalind's chestnut curls. "Let's stop by and say goodnight to Papa."

Sir Jason was propped up by a huge mound of down

pillows, reading a book and sipping what Callie was relatively sure was the smuggler's gift of brandy. At the girls' entrance, he put down the brandy, removed his steel-rimmed glasses, and beamed at them.

"Come in. Come in and let me look at you. My goodness, how those dresses take me back." He sighed. "That gown you have on, Diana, was one of your mother's. She wore it on our honeymoon." He looked off into the distance as if watching a scene from long ago. "She looked like an angel in it."

"What about mine, Papa?" Rosalind asked him.

"Hmmm." He studied the rose-velvet creation carefully. "I can't honestly say that I remember it, but whoever it belonged to would have been pleased with how well you become it," he added gallantly. "Now, your gown, Callie, I'll never forget." He gazed thoughtfully at the orange dress, noting the deeply cut neckline with its feather boa trim. The tight bodice emphasized her tiny waist, and the full skirt billowed out, camouflaging her thinnesss, while the brilliant hue highlighted the purity of her ivory complexion and brought out glints of red in her brown hair. "Your Grandmother Whitlaw was wearing it the night I came to ask for your mother's hand. I was so nervous that I spilled my tea on it, down by the bottom." He looked toward the elaborately ruffled hem.

"So that's what that stain was." Callie laughed. "We wondered."

"What about mine, Papa?" Olivia asked. "Do you remember mine?"

"No." Sir Jason studied the blue silk sack gown carefully. "But, if I'm not mistaken, that's the dress your great-aunt Harriet was wearing when she had her portrait painted."

"Great-aunt Harriet." Callie frowned, trying to place the name.

"You never met her, nor did I for that matter. She married a younger son and went to the Colonies before I was born. Her portrait is in the library. Now run along and have a good time, girls." He beamed at them. "I imagine Olivia can't wait to see Emmet again." He chuckled at Olivia's flush, totally misunderstanding the reason for her discomfiture. "I know, I'm a wicked old man to tease you so. Come, kiss me goodnight, and then you can go."

By the time they reached the Vardens', they were numb with the cold, despite the fact that Callie had insisted they bundle up in their warmest pelisses and hoods.

"Callie, you're half-frozen!" Ada greeted them at the door.

"We had to come in the landaulet." Callie sneezed as the warmth of the room hit her. "The closed carriage broke an axle last fall, and I haven't had it fixed yet."

"You can take our carriage home tonight," Gervais, who was standing behind Ada, said. "Your groom can bring it back in the morning when he gets yours."

"Thank you, Gervais." Callie smiled gratefully at him and thought, not for the first time, what a nice man he was.

"My pleasure. We can't have Abner's godmother down with a chill. In you go, and have a good time." He dismissed them as some new arrivals entered.

Callie shepherded her sisters into the ballroom at the back of the house and paused inside the doorway of the crowded room to peer at the guests. Not even to herself would she admit that she was looking for Rutledge, but he wasn't to be seen.

Despite the impossibility of obtaining fresh flowers and potted palms at this season, the ballroom was brilliantly colorful from the lavish costumes. Hundreds of candles in crystal chandeliers overhead illuminated the rich shades of the dancing guests' clothes. To the right of the door, a five-piece orchestra from Brighton was playing, and on the left side of the room, the wall was lined with chairs for those who preferred to watch the festivities rather than dance.

"Emmet Hadley is here!" Olivia hissed. "Quick, let's sit down before he notices us."

"There are some vacant chairs over there." Callie nodded toward the far side of the room. "But don't rush or he'll think you're upset."

"I am!" Olivia wailed. "How dare he come and spoil my evening!"

"It would have been an insult to Ada if he hadn't come," Callie pointed out. "After all, he was to dinner here just the other night, so he can hardly say he isn't up to socializing yet."

"Good evening, ladies," a deep voice greeted them and Callie's breath caught in her throat as she glanced sideways right into Rutledge's eyes. Those eyes glowed suddenly with a silvery light as he studied the firm swell of her breasts rising above the feather boa.

Callie studied his own costume, blinking at the magnificence of it. His tall frame was garbed in the full ball dress of fifty years ago. Green and gold lacing highlighted a green velvet coat. There was a profusion of fine lace at his wrists and throat, and a light dress sword around his waist completed the outfit. The very elaborateness of the costume served to emphasize his masculinity. Callie forced down her remembrance of the feel of that hard body pressed against hers and managed to respond to his greeting.

"Good evening, my lord, Mr. Kershaw," Callie acknowledged the earl and his ward, who nodded shyly at her. "I don't believe you've met my youngest sister, Rosalind. Rosalind, this is the Earl of Rutledge."

"I'm pleased to meet you, my lord." Rosalind curtsied, while Callie held her breath, fearful that the unpredictable hoops might fly up. Fortunately, they didn't.

"And I you, Miss Sutcliff." Rutledge bowed over Rosalind's hand as if she had been a duchess instead of a fourteen-year-old girl. "May I have the pleasure of this dance?"

"Oh, yes!" Rosalind bubbled, her little face alight with pride. "That'd be grand. None of my friends have ever danced with a real-live earl before," she added ingenuously.

"And this one certainly is alive." Callie smiled at Rutledge, her quip in no way disguising her gratitude at the pleasure he was giving her little sister.

"May I dance with Miss Diana, Miss Sutcliff?" Mr. Kershaw blurted out and then blushed bright red.

"You'd do better to ask her yourself." Callie pressed her twitching lips together firmly, determined not to laugh at the poor boy's embarrassment. Evidently Rutledge had instructed him to keep Diana occupied until he got back from his dance with Rosalind.

"Would you care to dance, Miss Diana?" He threw the question in Diana's general direction.

"Yes, please." Diana's softly voiced answer was barely audible, but Mr. Kershaw must have taken her assent for granted because he grabbed her arm and hurried her over to the set which was forming for a country dance.

"Mesdemoiselles?" D'Armagnac stopped Callie and Olivia before they reached the chairs. "It is to see you again a delight," the Frenchman said, practically oozing charm. "Might I have the pleasure of this dance, Miss Olivia? We will just find . . ." He looked around for a partner for Callie, his manners too good to leave her standing by herself.

"Oh, no," Callie refused when she realized his attention. "I'd much rather sit and watch the dancers. I'm here to chaperon my sisters."

"It is to joke, Miss Sutcliff. You are much too young to chaperon anyone, but if that is your wish, then allow us to escort you to your seat."

"Thank you." Callie nodded and followed meekly along beside them to the chairs. She sat down and then watched Olivia and d'Armagnac join the same set as Rosalind and the earl.

"Why so pensive, Callie?" Emmet slipped into the empty seat beside her.

"Oh, hello, Emmet," Callie greeted him abstractly. "I was just thinking."

"About d'Armagnac?" he guessed.

"Yes. Doesn't he strike you as rather . . . rather . . ." She fumbled for words.

"He's French," Emmet said as if that excused a lot.

"But what does he do?"

"Works in the War Office with the Horse Guards. He has a very responsible position, Callie, and he's very knowledgeable. I was discussing our Spanish campaign with him after dinner the other night."

"It seems rather strange to have a Frenchman working in the War Office." Callie frowned at his dancing figure.

"Not at all. He wants to defeat Napoleon every bit as badly as we do. Once the empire falls, d'Armagnac stands to regain considerable estates. He has much more cause to hate Napoleon than we do."

"Perhaps, but if he's all that smart, how did he get mixed up with Tristam?"

"Perhaps he isn't." Emmet shrugged. "He could simply have used Tristam to get a few weeks in the country. I don't think d'Armagnac has much money. At least, he doesn't dress like it."

"Poor, but proud. But not too proud to cadge a free stay at Ada's."

"Now, that's not really fair," Emmet defended the man. "You know as well as I do that Ada is overjoyed to have guests."

"Especially the earl." Callie giggled. "I fully expect her to make a shrine out of his bedroom, complete with a plaque that says the Earl of Rutledge slept here."

"It would be more accurate if she added 'with Mrs. Parr' at the bottom of the plaque."

"Oh, come now." Callie kept her voice level despite the rush of jealousy she felt at Emmet's words. "Surely he wouldn't be having an affair with Mrs. Parr with her husband in the same house. By the way, where is he?"

"In the library, castaway," Emmet stated flatly.

"I don't think I've ever seen him completely sober."

"I doubt that he ever is, but God knows that flighty piece he married would drive any man to drink."

"That's what happens when a man is stupid enough to marry a pretty face instead of what's behind the face." Callie refused to sympathize with Mr. Parr.

"You're beginning to sound like your grandmother as well as dress like her," Emmet teased her.

"It's true," Callie insisted. "Men fall in love with a pretty face and marry it, and then blame the woman when she doesn't conform to all their preconceived notions about her."

"Are you trying your hand at a spot of matchmaking, Callie?" Emmet eyed her narrowly. "You wouldn't be thinking of pushing Olivia in d'Armagnac's direction, would you?"

About to deny it hotly, Callie thought better of it. Why not let Emmet think that's what she was doing? At least then he wouldn't think poor Olivia was sitting at home pining for him. "Why not?" she asked.

"Why not!" Emmet exploded and then lowered his voice hastily as several people turned to stare. "For one thing, he's a Frenchie and for another, he's poor. Olivia needs to marry someone who can afford to buy her all the luxuries she deserves."

"And where is she supposed to find this paragon?" Callie inquired. "You're the only unmarried man in the neighborhood who fits that description, and you're already spoken for."

"You could take her to London for a season."

"With what?" Callie snapped. "We are quite literally all to pieces. We haven't a spare shilling, and, even if I could get her to London, it wouldn't do any good because she hasn't a dowry. None of us do. And, if anything happens to Papa, we won't even have a home. Cousin Joan has already served notice that we won't be welcome at The Meadings after Gilmer inherits."

"But . . ." Emmet sounded shaken.

"But nothing!" Callie interrupted him ruthlessly. "Under the circumstances, Olivia will be lucky if she can find a husband—any husband, even a poor Frenchman. And, if you were any kind of friend at all, you'd help her bring him up to scratch."

"Not likely!" Emmet glared furiously at her.

"Oh, Callie," Rosalind's excited voice broke into the tense silence following Emmet's outburst. "It was so much fun!"

Callie turned to Rosalind in relief. She'd gotten more of a reaction from Emmet than she'd expected with her probing, and she wasn't quite sure just what to make of it. It could be, of course, that Emmet was merely expressing concern for an old friend, but somehow that didn't ring true.

Diana was also an old friend, and he hadn't even noticed that Rutledge seemed to be interested in her.

"You danced very well, Rosalind," Callie praised her.

"Might I have the pleasure of the next dance, Rosalind?" Emmet got up. "That is, if you don't mind my empty sleeve?"

"Of course not. I'd like to dance with you." Rosalind beamed at him. "What kind of dance . . ." She broke off as the music started and her face fell. "Oh, Emmet, I can't. It's a waltz and I can't waltz because if you waltz before one of the patronesses of Almack's gives you permission, people will say you're fast. And I don't want to be fast."

"Too true." Emmet treated her concern with great gravity. "A young woman can't be too careful of her reputation. What say you that we go out into the kitchen and see what they're planning for refreshments?"

"Yes." Rosalind took his one arm and went off happily with him.

"A nice lad," Rutledge commented, claiming Emmet's vacant seat.

"Um-hum." Callie closed her eyes briefly and willed her speeding heart to stop its erratic pounding. It frightened her that she, who had always been so self-possessed, could be thrown into such confusion by Rutledge's mere appearance. It was because he was so vital to their plans, she told herself, trying hard to believe it.

"Not at all the type one would expect to raise his voice to a lady," Rutledge probed.

"No, he isn't and that's what makes it all the more interesting." Ignoring Rutledge's obvious curiosity, Callie changed the subject. "Where's Diana?"

"With James." The earl followed her lead. "Would you care to dance?"

"Thank you for asking me, but it's not necessary."

"No, but it might be fun."

"I doubt it." Callie grinned. "I'm a terrible dancer."

"Strange," he mused, "that someone with your talent for singing wouldn't have a sense of rhythm, too."

"Yes, isn't it?" Callie said wryly. She strongly suspected that he was making a May game of her, but she wasn't positive, and she lacked the conviction to confront him with his duplicity.

"May I compliment you on your choice of gown," Rutledge said, apparently deciding another topic of conversation was in order. "The color becomes you, and I've always liked feathers." His eyes lingered on the round swell of her breasts visible through the boa.

"Really, my lord!" Callie felt obligated to register an objection even though she was inordinately pleased that he found her figure praiseworthy.

"Yes, really," Rutledge assured her with a straight face. "Although I can't say that it's all the feathers."

"I meant that you shouldn't say such things!" Callie snapped. "It's not...not..." She searched wildly for a word and finally settled on the anemic "polite."

"Not polite?" Rutledge's black eyes gleamed with devilment. "How can it not be polite to tell a lady that you admire her?"

"You don't admire *me!*" Callie glared at him. "You admire my—" She broke off in horror as she realized what she'd almost blurted out.

"Feathers," Rutledge inserted with an engaging grin. "Of course, the fact that you have such lovely white skin to set them off doesn't hurt."

"You mustn't say such things." Callie shot a hasty glance around to make sure they hadn't been overheard, but no one was near enough.

"But why should I be mealymouthed and compose odes to your left eyebrow, when what I really like is your—"

"Quiet!" Callie hissed with another hasty look around to make sure no one had overheard him.

"Feathers." He looked at her in all innocence. "You seem very distraught tonight, Aunt Callie. Are you given to missish attacks?"

"No, I am not," Callie snapped, "and neither am I given to attacks of such blatant outspokenness. I would prefer you to change the subject."

"Very well. What caused Rosalind's lameness?" Rutledge shot the question at Callie.

"What!" Callie sounded as astonished as she felt.

"I'm perfectly aware that, according to the social conventions, one is supposed to pretend that one doesn't notice, but ignoring a problem doesn't help it."

"No, but it allows a person to lead at least some semblance of a normal life," Callie countered. "It isn't Rosalind's fault that she's lame."

"I didn't say it was," Rutledge replied, "and do stop responding like a broody hen with one chick. I asked because I like the child, not out of vulgar curiosity. It's possible that she could be helped."

"No, it isn't," Callie stated flatly. "Our doctor said that there's nothing to be done. She caught the withering fever five years ago. Her left arm is also affected."

"Forgive me for suggesting it, my dear, but a village doctor is not the best authority. She ought to be seen by Knighton in London."

Callie pressed her lips together for fear of what she might say and deliberately studied the gyrations of the gaily-colored dancers. She was well aware of Dr. Adams's limitation, but she was equally aware of the expense involved in seeking an opinion from one of the eminent London practitioners, even supposing she could get an appointment with him. "Sir William Knighton couldn't be bothered to see just anyone who came in from the provinces."

"I'm not criticizing you, Aunt Callie," Rutledge addressed her averted face. "I'm trying to help."

"Then you'd do well to remember that not everyone has your wealth or influence!" Callie gulped, horrified at the way her voice shook.

"Miss Callie, my lord," the Reverend Marston greeted them effusively.

For once, Callie was glad to see the vicar, and she turned to him in relief at the interruption.

"Good evening, Vicar." She eyed his garish costume with dismay. Dressed in a pink-and-white striped waistcoat and a rusty small sword held on by a bright blue sash, he looked ludicrous. "What a perfect example of Georgian dress," she finally said.

"Yes, isn't it?" Marston patted the elaborate fall of dusty lace under his plump chin complacently. "I rather pride myself on its authenticity. I picked it up when I was in Brighton yesterday. Yours looks excellent, too, my lord." Marston addressed the silent Rutledge with determined joviality. "Such line, such cut. I declare it quite puts mine to the blush, but then one would expect an earl's to be superior."

"I'm afraid the credit will have to go to my hostess," Rutledge responded dryly. "She allowed me scavenger rights to her attics."

"One would never guess that it wasn't tailored especially for you." Marston refused to be sidetracked from his toadying. "You're obviously a truly discerning man."

"You'd be amazed at just how discerning." Rutledge's sardonic voice caused Callie to shift in embarrassment, although Marston seemed to find nothing insulting in the earl's tone.

"And it's because you're so discerning that I wanted to talk to you," Marston continued, "about a matter that must concern you deeply. The church."

"No." Rutledge looked blandly into Marston's perspiring face.

"No?" Marston repeated, obviously confused. "But all peers are vitally concerned with the church."

"All I can say, Marston, is that your knowledge of peers is nil."

"Yes, but," Marston tried again, "I mean, you must appoint the livings on your estates."

"No," Rutledge repeated.

"But if you don't, who does?" Marston demanded.

"The bishop, of course. He's much more aware of the qualifications of the various clergy in his bishopric that I am. Why"—Rutledge warmed to his theme—"if I were to appoint the livings, I would probably have to fall back on appointing friends, and think of what disastrous repercussions such blatant favoritism could have on the holy church." Rutledge's pious voice made Callie want to laugh.

"How laudable!" Callie smiled at him. "How truly worthy of you to give up one of your privileges for the good of the church. Don't you think so, Vicar?" Callie fixed a questioning eye on the dejected Marston.

"Yes." Marston roused himself enough to agree and then, mumbling something about having to see Squire Varden on a matter of some importance, he scuttled off.

Callie tried to frown at the earl, but her sense of the ridiculous betrayed her, and she was unable to stop the laughter which bubbled over. "Horrid man. Have you no sense of shame? Don't you realize you've blighted all the poor man's hopes, and mine too, come to that?"

"I have the greatest dislike of people who toady in the hope that I'll give them something. Marston deserved to have his hopes blighted, but I fail to see how it should affect you."

"It stands to reason that if you appoint him to a living in Northumberland, he won't be here haranguing us every Sunday about our shortcomings."

"A subject that ought to give him plenty of raw material to work with." Rutledge's twinkling eyes took the sting out of the words. "Cheer up, Aunt Callie. Perhaps he'll—"

"Theron, dear," Mrs. Parr's seductive voice cut in. "There you are. I've been looking all over for you."

"Have you?" The earl looked amused, although he did rise and give Mrs. Parr his seat. "Now you've found us. Miss Sutcliff, you remember Mrs. Parr?" He turned politely to Callie.

"Um, yes." Callie tore her mesmerized gaze away from Mrs. Parr's incredible dress and searched frantically for a platitude. None revealed itself and she remained tongue-tied.

"How do you like my dress?" Mrs. Parr ran her hand sensuously over the silky material.

Callie stole an embarrassed glance at the creation and spared a thought to wonder if Mrs. Parr's grandmother had been a doxy. The low-cut dress consisted of a skirt and bodice with elaborate sleeves that ended at the elbow in a series of *engageantes*. But the tour de force was the transparent insert in the bodice through which the rouged tips of her breasts showed clearly.

"It's very unusual," Callie finally blurted out. "We found nothing like that in our attics."

"I should hope not!" Mrs. Parr sounded affronted. "My grandmother was French."

"I knew there must be a reason for it," Callie replied vaguely, keeping her eyes fixed firmly on Mrs. Parr's exquisite facial features.

Clearly uninterested in Callie, Mrs. Parr stood up and turned back to the earl. "Theron, dear," she purred, "do take me away from this appalling group of provincials. Please?" She moved closer to him until her barely covered breasts were rubbing against the front of his velvet coat.

"Good heavens, how remiss of us!" Callie exclaimed in simulated horror. "To allow you to become bored. I imagine you're just dying for an intelligent conversation with someone. But it's really very naughty of you to assume that 'Theron, dear'"—Callie shot the earl an acid glance—"is the only one among us who can amuse you. Why, I know just the person." Callie waved to the Reverend Marston, who was hovering in the background. "Oh, Reverend Marston," Callie trilled in a fair imitation of Ada at her vaguest, "do come and meet Mrs. Parr. Mrs. Parr," Callie swept on, ignoring the frozen look on the woman's face, "this is the Reverend Marston, our own very knowledgeable vicar. I'm sure there's nothing you could care to discuss that he wouldn't know about."

"But..." Mrs. Parr tried to force in a word.

"Nonsense, don't be shy," Callie rushed on. "The vicar will be pleased to see to your needs. Won't you, Reverend Marston?" Callie looked into the vicar's glazed eyes, which were riveted to Mrs. Parr's exposed bosom.

"But..." Mrs. Parr stuttered.

"You will excuse us." Callie grabbed the earl's arm and began to move away, forcing Rutledge to follow or else create a scene in an attempt to break away.

By the time they'd reached the morning room, Callie's

initial fury had subsided, and she let go of Rutledge's arm and risked a quick look up into his impassive face.

"Are we there?" he asked.

"Where?"

"Wherever it was that you were rushing me to."

"I'm sorry, my lord." Callie stared down at the green carpet.

"My lord?" Rutledge studied her embarrassed features. "A moment ago it was 'Theron, dear'."

"Yes," Callie muttered, "but she made me angry."

"That much was painfully obvious, madam, but, really, was it necessary to palm her off on Marston? Surely she couldn't have annoyed you that much?"

"It was rather severe." Callie's voice wobbled and she broke into laughter. "Did you see the horrified expression on her face?" she chortled. "And his? I doubt he's ever seen such a gown."

"You, my dear Aunt Callie, are a minx, and, if Mrs. Parr's gown upset you, you'd be permanently scandalized if you went to London."

"Since it's highly unlikely that I ever will, that's no problem. And if Mrs. Parr is a sample of London society, I can't say I'll miss it. But I am sorry if I upset a friend of yours."

Rutledge lightly traced a finger over the firm top of her creamy breast before his hand dipped down into the feather boa.

Callie's heart began to pound, and she was unable to suppress the shudder of sensual pleasure that shook her. Her reaction appeared to afford him considerable satisfaction. He stepped back as a wandering couple drifted into the room.

"Things are not always what they seem, Aunt Callie." Rutledge lightly flicked the end of her nose. "So don't leap to conclusions. Now, shall we find our various charges?"

And how was she meant to take that? Callie wondered as she obediently took his arm and accompanied him back toward the ballroom. Was he trying to tell her that he wasn't really a friend of Mrs. Parr's, or that the attention he was paying Diana didn't mean anything, or, perhaps he was just making idle conversation.

"My lord." Gervais' gruff voice stopped them as they reached the doorway of the ballroom. The squire hurried up to them, his plump body squeezed tightly into an elaborate Georgian outfit complete with a white wig from which a faint cloud of powder rose every time he moved his head.

Callie turned toward him, smiling as Ada rushed up behind him, her full hoops obviously giving her problems.

"My lord, you must come and meet some of my neighbors." Gervais' attitude to the earl was a curious blend of awe and cameraderie. As well it might be, Callie thought with an uneasy glance at Rutledge, remembering his cavalier treatment of the bootlicking Marston. Rutledge was not the sort of man one treated with undue familiarity. But, to Callie's unbounded relief, the earl seemed to see nothing amiss in being dragged off to be introduced to the locals as if he were some kind of oddity especially imported for the occasion.

"Miss Sutcliff." Rutledge nodded to Callie before he left with Gervais. "We never did have that dance. May I claim it later?"

"He's nice, even if he is rather grand," Ada said as she watched the earl and her husband disappear into the crowded ballroom.

"Yes." Callie's voice softened unconsciously. "He gave Rosalind the treat of her young life with that dance."

"Has he danced with Diana yet?"

"No, he appointed Mr. Kershaw her guardian before he danced with Rosalind, and then he sat out the next one with me."

"And Mrs. Parr!" Ada clicked her tongue in exasperation. "I never saw the like of the way she tried to annex him. Did you ever see such a disgraceful dress! And her breasts— why, she rouged them!" Ada's voice rose.

"Hush, Ada." Callie looked around quickly. "Someone will hear you."

"Hear me? What difference does it make if anyone hears me? They can all see."

"And what a view." Callie sighed. "I must admit I wish

I had more of her curves."

"She'll run to fat before she's thirty." Ada dismissed Mrs. Parr's figure with the wave of a hand. "What I wish is that she hadn't picked my ball to run around half-dressed. Whatever will people think?" Ada sounded truly worried.

"The obvious," Callie responded calmly. "That she's got the morals of a barn cat and is determined to seduce the earl."

"Calpurnia!"

"It's true," Callie insisted, unrepentant. "You should have seen the way she snuggled up to him, and in front of a whole room full of people. But I fixed her. I introduced her to the vicar."

"Oh, Callie, you didn't!" Ada stared at her friend, torn between admiration for such tactics and dismay at the thought of the consequences. "Now we'll probably have to listen to him spout about the sins of the flesh for the rest of the winter."

"Maybe." Callie grinned as she remembered his glassy-eyed stare. "But at the moment I doubt he's saying anything. He appeared to be stunned."

"That I would like to have seen, but right now I've got to go check on Mary. The poor lamb's teeth are still bothering her."

"I'll go for you," Callie offered. "I'm not all that fond of dancing."

"Nor that good," Ada retorted. "But I would appreciate your checking on the baby. I don't like to leave the ball, but I worry about her."

"Leave my goddaughter to me. We have an understanding. You go in and make polite noises like the excellent hostess you are." Callie started toward the back stairs.

"Oh, Callie," Ada called after her. "If she's restless, take some of the laudanum in the blue bottle on the mantel and rub a little on her gums, but don't let her drink any."

"Rub, don't drink," Callie repeated and then ran lightly up the stairs. The second floor was dark and silent as Callie made her way toward the stairs which led to the third floor nurseries. She rounded the corner and slammed into a tall, slim man, who jumped back at the collision.

"Tristam!" Callie looked at him in surprise. "Anyone looking at you would swear your grandfather was a clerk. Why aren't you at the ball? They're your guests."

"Um." Tristam jerked back farther into the shadows. "I've got a touch of the headache, and I thought a walk would cure it."

"A walk!" Callie peered closer at him, wondering if he were foxed. "It's snowing out there and it's cold enough to freeze your headache, never mind cure it."

"Good." Tristam laughed with nervous shrillness. "I'll be going then. If anyone asks after me, tell them I'll be down shortly, would you, Callie? I don't want anyone to rag me about my headache." He took two steps backward, turned and broke into a frank run.

"Headache, nothing!" Callie watched him go with cynical amusement. In all probability, he was on his way to a card game, and, from the stealthy way he was going about it, he didn't want his brother to know. Which undoubtedly meant he was losing, and, since Tristam never did anything by halves, he was probably losing in a big way. Shaking her head at Tristam's stupidity, Callie continued down the hall. There wasn't anything she could do to stop him, nor was she foolish enough to try.

- 8 -

CALLIE OPENED THE door to her father's room quietly and looked in, entering when she saw Sir Jason sitting up in bed reading.

"Good morning, Callie," he greeted her. "How was the ball last night?"

"Marvelous! Diana was a great success," she related with pride. "The earl danced twice with her and then had his ward spend most of the evening amusing her because the earl was in such demand that he couldn't stay with her."

"And, of course, Olivia spent the evening with Emmet," Sir Jason said.

"No one could doubt that she was aware of Emmet," Callie replied with perfect truth, remembering the feverish manner in which Olivia had flirted with the Frenchman, determined that Emmet should see that his defection hadn't bothered her in the least.

"May I get you anything, Papa?" Callie steered the conversation away from Olivia.

"No thank you, dear," Sir Jason answered absently, as he picked up his book again.

"I'll stop in later, then." Callie dropped a kiss on his pale cheek.

Downstairs she found Rosalind and Olivia in the morning room, huddled in front of a roaring fire drinking hot chocolate.

"Good morning, Rosalind." Callie smiled at her. "When did you get back from Ada's?"

"Just a few minutes ago. Mr. Kershaw brought me home in Ada's sleigh, and then he took Diana out for a ride."

"Was the earl with him?" Olivia asked the question Callie wanted to.

"No." Rosalind shook her head. "I didn't see him before I left Applewood this morning."

"Speaking of the earl . . ." Callie frowned slightly and perched on the edge of a worn blue damask chair.

"Yes?" Olivia prompted her.

"I'm beginning to have my doubts about our plan for nabbing him," Callie confessed.

"You don't think it'll work!" Rosalind demanded.

"Not exactly. I just think that our plan isn't quite broad enough."

"But we did everything just as they did in *Isabella's Quest*," Olivia protested.

"We knew that it couldn't possibly be that easy," Callie reminded them, "because, according to the book, all we had to do was to put the earl in the way of clapping eyes on Diana and he'd be smitten. But no rational man is going to propose marriage on the basis of one look."

"Perhaps not," Olivia admitted, "but he danced twice with her last night, which was more than he did with anyone else."

"It's obvious that he admires her looks, but that's not enough. We must get a declaration from him as soon as possible. He could leave for London at any time."

"I know," Olivia conceded gloomily, "but what else can we do? The plan worked for Isabella."

"Maybe we used the wrong book," Rosalind suggested.

Callie stared thoughtfully into the dancing flames for a moment before she replied. "You're right, Rosalind. We should have used lots of ideas instead of pinning all our hopes on one method. Something is bound to work. We simply need to find it."

"But you can't deny that our plan has caught the earl's interest," Olivia insisted.

Callie ignored the shaft of pain that tore through her at hearing Olivia's confirmation of Rutledge's interest in Diana. She closed her mind to everything but the absolute necessity of capturing the earl. Her sisters had to be provided for no matter what the cost to her heart.

"I don't deny it," Callie said, "but now that we've managed to fix his interest, we need something to force a declaration. But what?"

"Remember *The Last Marquis?*" Rosalind bounced on the sofa in excitement, almost spilling her hot chocolate.

"Vaguely." Callie frowned. "Didn't he get married to save his estates?"

"No," Rosalind corrected, "that was *The Wicked Duke*. The last marquis got married because his mother died and he needed a hostess."

"I remember," Olivia enthused. "A hostess should be very important to an earl. Peers do lots of entertaining."

"All that we have to do is to show him that Diana would make him a marvelous society hostess," Rosalind said.

"That's easier said than done." Callie sighed. "First of all, with Papa so sick, we can't give a large party here. And, secondly, Diana has never served as a hostess."

"This is hardly the time to cavil over trifles," Olivia dismissed Callie's worries. "We can use Papa's illness as an excuse to make the dinner party very small, just Ada and her guests. That way, Diana's lack of experience won't be quite so obvious."

"I still don't like it," Callie insisted.

"Neither do I," Olivia said, "but what choice have we?"

"None," Callie answered honestly. "We have to broaden our plan to appeal to the earl, and acquiring a competent hostess should certainly appeal to a man in his position. I can prompt Diana on her role, and we can both stay close to her to make sure nothing goes wrong."

"What could go wrong?" Rosalind asked with all the enthusiasm of youth. Callie merely smiled, seeing no reason to elaborate on the myriad pitfalls awaiting a shy, inexperienced girl trying to convince someone as knowledgeable as the earl that she was up to every move on the social board.

"It might work, Callie," Olivia said. "As smitten as he seems to be, he won't be looking for perfection."

"No, he won't," Callie agreed with effort, trying to ignore the fact that it was becoming harder and harder to enter wholeheartedly into their efforts to effect the earl's capture.

"Do you have any other ideas for enlarging our plan?" Callie looked hopefully at her two sisters. "Every little nudge in the right direction brings him closer to the precipice."

"Sometimes the hero marries to have an heir," Rosalind suggested.

"True," Olivia nodded, "especially someone in the earl's position."

"Granted," Callie said dryly, "but how would you propose we go about it? Casually bring the conversation around to children and then suggest that he isn't getting any younger and he ought to look to the succession?"

"Not me!" Olivia shuddered. "The earl is not the type of man with whom one takes liberties, and that would most definitely be a liberty."

"Exactly," Callie said. "There really isn't any way to bring it up tactfully. And it's a shame because that's a very common reason for marriage among peers."

"Can't you think of anything else, Callie?" Olivia asked.

"There was that book we read last winter," Callie said slowly. "Something about a great heiress who ran away rather than marry the wicked rake her greedy stepfather had promised her to."

"I remember!" Rosalind cried. "She disguised herself as a boy and a duke made her his page, and she shared all his adventures, and in the end he married her because she was such a great gun!"

"That doesn't sound much like Diana," Olivia said uncertainly. "She can't even ride a horse sidesaddle, let alone astride. Hunting scares her, and she'd probably faint at the first sign of a mill."

"A definite disadvantage." Callie laughed. "But I think that the main thing the duke meant was that she was willing to share his interests and that she was game for anything—not that she did things as well as a man."

"Whatever." Olivia shrugged. "It hardly matters since Diana isn't game for anything, nor does she share any of his interests—except possibly dancing."

"It isn't important what she really thinks," Callie insisted. "All that matters is what the earl perceives her interests to be."

"I guess so," Olivia conceded, "but how do you plan on convincing him that Diana shares his interests?"

"I don't know," Callie said, "but I think we ought to add the idea to our plan just in case. We can't afford to overlook anything. We can hold it in reserve in case the hostess idea doesn't succeed."

"Or the heir," Rosalind said.

"Unfortunately, I'm afraid we're going to have to admit defeat on that idea, Rosalind," Callie said.

"Never mind," Olivia consoled her. "We know he's wavering. The hostess plan should be enough to push him over the edge."

"I hope so," Callie said, overwhelmed by the desolate feeling that engulfed her at Olivia's words. A feeling she steadfastly refused to allow into her conscious thoughts, instinctively knowing that it would only make a bad situation worse.

The dinner party was arranged for the following evening, since all four sisters were agreed that speed was of the essence. Unfortunately, their haste made it impossible to fashion a new gown for Diana, so they compromised by changing the pink ribbons on her new white dress to violet ones which deepened the blue of Diana's eyes. They arranged her golden hair into a high knot on the top of her head, with short ringlets cascading over her ears.

About her own gown, Callie could not afford to be so
fastidious. She merely slipped on a turquoise dress that she'd
rescued from the attic. She felt a momentary flash of envy
as she caught sight of herself and Diana reflected in the
morning-room mirror as they awaited their guests. Diana
looked so fresh and lovely, dressed in the height of fashion,
while Callie looked like a poor relation. They'd all be poor
relations if she couldn't manage to bring this plan to fruition,
Callie told herself grimly, and leaned over to give yet another hint to the frightened Diana.

Callie's first intimation that things were not going to run
according to plan came before dinner, when Diana, after a
cursory greeting of her guests, settled herself on the sofa
beside James Kershaw and engaged him in conversation,
leaving the way clear for Mrs. Parr to monopolize Rutledge.
And the earl seemed to have no objection, Callie noted with
annoyance.

She tried to catch Diana's eye to remind her of her duties,
but the only person Diana was looking at was James Kershaw. Callie could have screamed in vexation. She knew
that she'd told Diana that it was a good idea to be on
excellent terms with Rutledge's ward, but she hadn't meant
to the exclusion of the earl himself!

Dinner gave the sisters more scope to expand Diana's
role as hostess, mainly due to Callie's foresight in the seating
arrangements. Mrs. Parr had been placed as far away from
Rutledge as possible, leaving Diana in uncontested posses-
sion of his attention. Unfortunately, Diana did nothing to
foster her image as a society hostess. Instead of amusing
the earl with witty *on dits*, she blushed and stammered her
way through both courses.

As soon as the table had been cleared, Callie nodded to
Diana to signal her to lead the ladies out and leave the men
to their port.

"You look tired, Callie." Ada sat down beside her friend.

"I think 'drained' might be a better word for it. We had
such hopes for this evening, too. It was a perfect chance to
show Rutledge what a great hostess Diana could be, and
look what happened. She behaved like a shy young bud."

"Which she is," Ada pointed out reasonably.

"I know." Callie sighed. "It was bird-witted of us to expect that a few hints could turn Diana into a poised hostess when she's never so much as presided over a tea party."

"Perhaps we could try again later," Ada suggested. "Maybe all she needs is practice."

"Undoubtedly, but there simply isn't time enough for her to get it. The earl could leave at any time, and we were counting on this dinner to provide the impetus for him to declare himself. I know his affections are engaged," Callie insisted. "He just needs a final push."

"He certainly isn't backward in his attentions to Diana, and he has his ward guard her when he can't be there. But I think the hostess idea was a bad one, Callie. Your first notion was inspired. Diana really is a diamond of the first water, and he was bound to realize it just by looking at her. By the same token, she isn't an accomplished hostess, and he was bound to discover that, too."

"You're right, of course, but it was worth a try."

"Although maybe we're giving up too soon," Ada amended. "Can you tell Diana again what she should be doing?"

"She'll cry," Callie stated with flat certainty. "The least hint of criticism has always upset her so. You know what tender feelings she has." Callie paused as the hair on the back of her neck prickled. Instinctively, she knew that Rutledge had entered the room. It was uncanny the way her body was becoming attuned to his very presence. She looked across the room to where Diana was fingering the old spinet, willing her to greet him.

"Excuse me, Callie." Ada got up hurriedly. "I want to tell Gervais something."

Callie watched surreptitiously as Rutledge paused in the doorway, looked over at his hostess beside the spinet, and then walked leisurely to the sofa and sat down beside Callie.

"Good evening, Aunt Callie," he greeted her.

"My lord." Callie stole a quick look at Diana, but she was now deep in conversation with James Kershaw. Dash it! Callie could have screamed. How were they ever going to make their plan work if Diana kept forgetting the role assigned to her? Drawing a deep breath, Callie prepared to advance her sister's cause.

"Diana is certainly in looks tonight," she said.

"Diana is always in looks," he replied carelessly, "which is more than can be said for you." He studied her somber gown with evident distaste. "You looked much better in feathers."

"I'm not a bird, my lord!" Callie snapped, hurt by his uncomplimentary comparison of her to Diana, even though she tried to tell herself that she ought to be overjoyed that he saw Diana as the ideal women.

"Certainly not a ladybird." He grinned at her.

Callie pressed her lips together and refused to dignify his sally with a response, although she was unable to suppress the images which flooded her mind at the thought of being a ladybird. Of being his ladybird. Of being able to touch him whenever she pleased, of being able to run her fingers through his curly black hair, of being able to press her lips against his, of being able to... She clamped down hastily on her wayward thoughts and turned to Rosalind, who had joined them.

"Good evening, Miss Rosalind," Rutledge greeted her and smiled as the young girl beamed at him. "Please sit down." He moved closer to Callie to give her sister room on the sofa.

Callie tried to shift away from the disturbing feel of his hard body pressed against her, but the end of the sofa cut off her escape.

"Winters are so wretched!" Rosalind said with a theatrical sigh. "I don't get out much, but I do like to read. Do you?"

"Yes," the earl said.

"I thought you would," Rosalind nodded sagely, "so I brought you a book to read."

For the first time Callie noticed that Rosalind was holding a slim black-leather volume. Callie blinked, looked again, and was filled with a horrible sense of foreboding. Surely Rosalind wouldn't.

"It's a trump. It's called the *The Lonely Duke,* and it's

all about a duke who needs to get married because he doesn't have a son."

"Rosalind," Callie said, trying to head her younger sister off. But Rosalind hurried on.

"It's very important for a duke to have a son," Rosalind belabored the point, "and earls, too. Have you got a son?"

"The earl isn't married, Rosalind," Callie broke in.

"The one does not necessarily preclude the other," Rutledge commented, his black eyes twinkling at Callie.

"What?" Rosalind demanded.

"No, child," Rutledge said. "I don't have any sons. Or daughters, either, come to that."

"Then you should," Rosalind told him. "Think of what would happen if you died. It'd be too late then."

"So I've been told," Rutledge replied gravely, although Callie felt laughter shake his large frame—laughter Callie felt was totally heartless. She knew it was imperative to break up the conversation, but she very much feared that the only way to do so would be to physically restrain Rosalind. And that would alert Rutledge to just how upset Callie was. Far better to try to stop Rosalind gently, pretending that it was simply childish interest which had prompted her words.

"I'll definitely have to marry before I die," Rutledge agreed with the young girl.

"Rosalind—" Callie tried.

"You don't want to leave it too late." Rosalind ignored her sister. "You might get too old. When you're too old—"

"Rosalind!" Callie threw caution to the wind and halted the conversation, no matter what conclusions Rutledge drew. There was no telling what else Rosalind might blurt out, given more time. "It's late, Rosalind. Say goodnight to the earl."

"Good night, my lord." Rosalind smiled happily at Callie, as if she'd just managed to solve all their problems singlehandedly. "Don't forget to read the book." Rosalind thrust the volume into his hands, and, with a final sunny smile at Callie, left.

Callie closed her eyes and swallowed. "You must forgive Rosalind, my lord. She's become very romantic lately."

"Romantic?" Rutledge questioned. "To marry to secure the succession? That hardly seems romantic to me. More practical than anything else."

"Yes, well . . ." Callie licked her dry lips and eyed him uncertainly.

"Of course, there's a flaw in her reasoning," Rutledge continued meditatively. "What if I married and the union proved barren? Then the whole exercise would have been a waste."

"That is in the hands of God," Callie snapped, "and this whole discussion is most improper."

"Securing the succession?" Rutledge looked surprised.

"Not securing the succession, but how you intend to do it!"

"I wasn't aware that there was more than one way to secure a succession, Aunt Callie, but I'm always willing to learn."

"No doubt. I've noticed your thirst for knowledge!"

"For teaching." His twinkling black eyes mocked her embarrassment.

Callie pressed her lips together, admitting to herself the impossibility of fencing verbally with him. He was a past master at the art of social repartee. It was far more dignified to refuse to be drawn.

"I am persuaded you wouldn't enjoy the book," Callie said firmly and reached for it, but Rutledge refused to let go.

"It might while away an hour or two. Rosalind was correct about the winter's limiting one's choice of activities."

"If you want to read a book, I'd be pleased to lend you one of my Papa's," Callie suggested. "It will be much more to your tastes than a gothic novel."

"Perhaps. Shall we see?" Rutledge stood up and Callie blinked uncertainly at him.

"See?"

"See the library. Since Diana is acting the hostess this

evening, you won't be missed for the short time it should take me to choose a book."

Callie frowned suspiciously at his reference to Diana's abortive role as hostess, but his lean face was devoid of expression.

"Yes." Callie decided her only viable option was to accept his words at face value. "Diana is practicing her role as hostess. Of course, she's just learning," Callie rushed on when she saw him glance over to where Diana was talking to James Kershaw and ignoring the rest of her guests, "but given a few years, I'm sure she'll be a brilliant society hostess."

"Quite a few," Rutledge said dryly, and Callie wisely allowed the subject to drop.

The library was dark and Callie quickly lit several candles from the small fire burning in the grate. Unfortunately, they didn't illuminate the room evenly, but rather served to accentuate the shadows, creating an aura of intimacy.

"Now then," Callie's brisk voice purposefully rejected the atmosphere, "what do you like?"

"Well," Rutledge drawled as his eyes ran over her slim figure.

"In books!" Callie bit out. She turned to the orderly shelves filled with leather-bound volumes.

"What could rival a book about a duke and his problems over the succession?" Rutledge looked down at the black-covered novel he still held.

"Burke's Peerage!"

Rutledge appeared to consider her suggestion, and then shook his head. "Too dry. Do you have any other ideas?"

"Certainly. Papa received an order just the other day from Hatchard's in London." Callie studied the shelves a moment and then remembered where she'd put it. She moved the library steps over and climbed up on them.

"Here you are." She pulled a thick brown tome out. "Wolf's *Prolegomena ad Homerum*," Callie read, mutilating the Latin title. "Papa said it was fascinating. Although I don't see how anything with a title like that could possibly be fascinating," she added thoughtfully.

"It helps if you can read Latin," Rutledge replied dryly.

"Perhaps," Callie replied doubtfully. "Here." She started to climb back down the steps, caught her slipper in the hem of her over-long skirt, and, to her horror, tumbled off, falling to the floor.

The earl was beside her instantly. "Poor Aunt Callie," he murmured catching her up in his arms then seating himself on the sofa, cradling her trembling body close to the comforting warmth of his hard chest. Callie hadn't been hurt by the fall, and wasn't sure why she *was* trembling. She did realize that sitting on the earl's lap was a much too intimate position, and that she should move, but she truly didn't want to. The earl tipped her face up and studied it momentarily, his eyes softening as her own widened with confusion. He lowered his head and gently kissed each eyelid, trailing kisses down her cheek to the corner of her soft pink mouth.

Callie's breath caught in her throat as the touch of his lips sent a flood of feeling through her. She squirmed restlessly on his lap, suddenly aware of the firmness of his muscular thighs and chest where they pressed into her soft flesh. She drew a shaky breath as his wandering lips began a leisurely exploration of the sensitive hollow behind her left ear. Callie nervously licked her dry lips and attempted to rally her thoughts, which seemed to be drowning in a sea of sensual feeling. This was all wrong, she tried to tell herself. Rutledge was for Diana. He shouldn't be making casual love to her.

"No," she moaned, "you mustn't . . ." But the rest of her sentence was lost as his lips closed over hers. His arms tightened, crushing her soft breasts against the slightly scratchy feel of his coat while his hands caressed her back, molding her even closer to the hard contours of his body. His lips hardened and exerted pressure, forcing hers to part. Immediately he deepened the kiss, his tongue invading and exploring the shape of her mouth.

Callie reacted mindlessly to the primitive urges that swept her, arching herself against him in an instinctive desire to prolong the intensity of feeling he was invoking. To her dismay, he broke off the kiss suddenly and turned her flushed face into the pristine whiteness of his neckcloth. Callie tried to protest, but one firm hand on the back of her head held her pressed there, while the other rhythmically rubbed her neck, helping to ease the tension he'd created.

Callie drew an unsteady breath as she tried to calm her whirling mind, but only one fact surfaced from the maelstrom of feeling. She loved Rutledge. Loved him and wanted him with all the fervor of a hitherto unsuspectedly passionate nature.

"I'm so sorry." Price's quavering voice broke into Callie's revery and she squirmed in embarrassment. Whatever must he think?

"It's quite all right, Price," Rutledge said. "Miss Sutcliff fell off the library steps while getting me a book. She was frightened, but she's fine now."

"Certainly, my lord," Price responded, obviously respecting the authority in the earl's voice. "I'll tend to the fire later."

Once Price had left, Callie forced herself to look up into Rutledge's calm face, searching hopelessly for some sign that the experience that had shaken her so had been equally meaningful to him. But except for a tiny reddish glow in the back of his ebony eyes, he looked his usual sophisticated self.

"Why did you do that?" she blurted out.

He smiled lazily at her, his eyes lingering on her softly swollen lips before he slipped an arm under her knees and lifted her gently off his lap, setting her down on the sofa beside him. "Because my nanny always used to say 'kiss and make it better.'" His voice was threaded with laughter.

"I see." Callie stood up, willing herself not to burst into tears at his prosaic response to what had been to her a soul-shattering experience. "Since you've found a book you want, we'd best rejoin the others, my lord."

"Certainly, Aunt Callie." His instant agreement depressed her even further. It was as if, having once kissed her, he had no further interest. And it was a good thing too, she lectured herself. The man was going to be her brother-in-law. Diana had to marry him, or all three of her beloved sisters were lost. That was what was important, Callie impressed upon herself. Nothing mattered except her sisters' futures and her father's peace of mind.

Once the last carriage had pulled away, Callie went back to the morning room to face Olivia and Diana. To her surprise, Rosalind was also there.

"I couldn't sleep," Rosalind explained, bouncing on the sofa. "Did he pay his addresses?"

"No!" Diana burst into tears. "I'm so sorry, Callie, but I kept forgetting what you told me to do."

"Don't cry, Diana," Callie said tiredly. "It takes years to learn to be a hostess. It was bird-witted of us to expect you to do it in a few hours."

"She's right, Diana," Olivia said. "It wasn't your fault that that portion of the plan didn't work. After all, it was only one part of our scheme."

"That's true," Callie comforted the tearful Diana. "And not even the most important part. No general expects everything to go his way. At least we showed the earl that you have potential and are willing to learn."

"Really?" Diana sniffed.

"Positively," Callie asserted, "and it might be best this way anyway. He can train you to be the type of hostess he wants."

"I took care of the next part of our plan," Rosalind broke in. "I reminded him about his duty to the succession, and then I gave him *The Lonely Duke* to read just in case he didn't fully understand," she finished triumphantly.

"You didn't!" Olivia stared at Rosalind in horror.

"It was all right, Livy," Rosalind assured her. "I was very sub, sut . . ."

"Subtle, dear," Callie supplied and then frowned quellingly at Olivia. There was nothing to be gained at this point by ranting at Rosalind for her ill-advised act. Rosalind thought she'd been helping, and, besides, she'd only been implementing an idea they'd all discussed. It wasn't Rosalind's fault that she was too young to have developed a little discretion.

"Once he reads it, he's bound to take the point," Rosalind enthused.

"We can always hope," Callie said. "Now off to bed, Rosalind. It's much too late for you to be up."

"Good night, Callie." Rosalind hugged her. "I'm so glad I had the idea to give him the book. I wanted to help, too."

Olivia waited until Rosalind, accompanied by Diana, had left the room before demanding, "Did she really?"

"Really," Callie sighed, "but I think I was able to pass it off as a young girl's romantic fancy." Callie kept her doubts to herself.

"Thank God for that! But what do we do now?"

"Well, we've tried all the ideas in our books except the idea of convincing the earl that Diana has all the same interests as he."

"Ha!" Olivia snorted. "If we couldn't even turn her into a mediocre hostess, how do you propose we turn her into a match for a sporting enthusiast?"

"Who reads things with long Latin titles." Callie shuddered.

"How do you know that?" Olivia demanded.

"I loaned him one of Papa's books to try to take his mind off Rosalind's offering, and that's what he chose."

"Daunting," Olivia admitted. "Diana can barely read English. What do we do next, Callie?"

"Let me think about it, Livy." Callie sighed despondently. "Something has to work. It's just a matter of finding it."

- 9 -

BY THURSDAY AFTERNOON, Callie was beginning to get desperate. Despite having put three-fourths of their plan into effect, Rutledge hadn't been to call since the evening of the dinner party, and, according to Ada, he spent his afternoons driving Mrs. Parr about the countryside. The only thing that hadn't caused Callie to give up hope entirely was the fact that Rutledge sent his ward around every day to keep Diana company. Such was the state of Callie's mind that she even briefly considered trying to trap the earl into a compromising situation, but the memory of his strength made her shiver, and she discarded the idea hastily. An indifferent husband was one thing, a hostile one something else again. Finally Callie decided to visit Ada in the hopes that her friend would be able to shed some light on Rutledge's intentions. She hadn't been there above five minutes when Johnston announced Emmet Hadley.

"Good afternoon, Emmet," Ada greeted the new arrival. "Johnston, please bring a fresh pot of tea."

"What brought you out in all this snow, Emmet?" Callie asked curiously.

"Just wanted to get out." Emmet cast a furtive glance around the room. "Are you by yourself, Callie?"

"Yes. Rosalind doesn't like the cold, and Mr. Kershaw and d'Armagnac came to visit, so Diana and Olivia stayed home."

"And you left them!" Emmet sounded outraged.

"My dear Emmet, Olivia is one-and-twenty, and Diana is eighteen, to say nothing of the fact that Papa is at home and the house is full of servants."

"Your father is a sick man, and the servants wouldn't interfere with Quality. Who knows what they might do!" Emmet seemed to be having trouble keeping his voice level.

"You mean they might try to seduce the girls to pass the time of day?" Callie eyed Emmet with amusement. "Oh, Emmet, think! James Kershaw is too shy to ever go beyond the line of what's pleasing."

"And what about that damn Frenchie?" Emmet ground out. "Is he so shy, too?"

"No," Callie appeared to be giving his words due consideration, "but he's definitely a gentleman. Perhaps it wouldn't be such a bad idea if he did seduce her, though then he'd have to marry her."

"Calpurnia!" Emmet jumped to his feet and glared furiously at her, his one hand clenching convulsively.

"Oh, sit down, Emmet." Callie lost interest in baiting him. "You sound like the father in a poorly written melodrama."

"That's all very well for you to say, but—"

"But she's my sister, Emmet. And, if I might remind you, your loyalties lie elsewhere, so cut line."

Emmet cast a quick look at the frankly curious Ada. "As you say, my loyalties lie elsewhere," he said stiffly before reseating himself.

"Tell us how to entertain the earl." Ada, always the peacemaker, changed the subject.

"Slip Mrs. Parr into his room," Emmet suggested.

"We want something original." Callie grinned at him.

"How about a skating party?" he asked. "The pond on my property is frozen over."

"We could light a bonfire, just as we used to do when we were young." Callie picked up on his idea with enthusiasm, quick to draw a parallel to Diana's graceful skating and the heroine who won the duke because she managed to convince him she shared his interest in sports.

"Can you two imagine Mr. Parr on skates?" Ada demanded.

"Not in a vertical position." Callie laughed. "But what difference could it possibly make to him? He can be cast away at Emmet's just as well as here."

"True," Ada admitted. "Maybe he won't even want to come. But what about skates? They won't have any."

"We can borrow some from the neighbors," Callie said. "They won't mind, but we'd best do it at once. We can't count on the snow lasting much longer. It's already been here five days."

"Yes." Ada tapped her fingers thoughtfully on the chair. "If we were to have the party tomorrow—say, in the afternoon—then you may invite us all to dinner, Emmet."

"Can I?" Emmet quizzed her.

"Of course you can. You've got a perfectly capable staff. Do them good to have something to do besides cater to one lone man. What you need is a wife and a family to enliven that old pile."

"Perhaps I do," Emmet replied evenly, his face carefully blank. "Then shall we say tomorrow at three unless I hear otherwise?" He stood up to take his leave.

"But you just got here." Ada seemed confused by his sudden desire to leave.

"Nevertheless, if I'm to have a houseful of guests tomorrow, I'd best start preparing now."

"I'll ride along with you, if you don't mind. It's time I was leaving also." Callie smiled slyly at him. "As you pointed out, my poor, defenseless sisters are at home alone and at the mercy of two scurrilous villains."

"I'll wait for you outside," Emmet snapped. "Good-bye, Ada. Thank you for the tea."

"But he didn't have any tea." Ada turned to Callie in perplexity after he'd left. "Do you think his injury could have affected his brain?"

"No." Callie stared thoughfully at the empty doorway. "Not his injury, but my scurrilous villains."

"Oh, well." Ada shrugged her plump shoulders. "I imagine someone will eventually tell me what's going on."

"Don't worry, Ada." Callie gave her a hug. "Just as soon as there's anything to tell, you'll be the first to know. Goodbye now. I'd best not keep Emmet waiting. In the mood he's in, he's liable to leave without me."

To Callie's infinite relief, Friday dawned crystal-clear and ice-cold, a perfect day for skating. Just why she was pinning so much hope on the day's excursion, she wasn't sure, but the party seemed vitally important to her. Time was definitely running out, and they had to get some kind of commitment from Rutledge soon or admit defeat. He'd already been there a week, and it was highly unlikely that he'd be willing to remain in rural Kent indefinitely, despite Mrs. Parr's undoubted charms. Once he was satisfied that his ward was recovering nicely, Rutledge would be bound to move on. A peer of the earl's rank and wealth would have invitations outstanding from far more important people than the Vardens.

By the time the sisters had gathered in the hallway to leave, Callie had worried herself into a nervous frazzle. Her head was pounding, her stomach was queasy, and all her anxieties were visible in her pale, pinched face.

"Are you all right, Callie?" Olivia, not usually the most perceptive of people, noticed her looks.

"Of course I am." Callie dismissed Olivia's concern. "Hurry up and get ready. Price said the pony trap would be here any minute. Just a second, Diana. Turn around and let me see how you look in that blue wool."

Diana held out her arms obediently and pirouetted, ending by overbalancing and having to grab hold of the banister to keep from falling.

"For heaven's sake, don't do that when you're on skates,"

Callie said. "I'm counting on your graceful figure impressing the earl because this skating party is the closest we're likely to come to convincing him that you share his interest in sports, and it had better succeed. Frankly, I've run out of ideas."

"Maybe Diana could manage to fall into the pond and then the earl could rescue her," Rosalind suggested from the bottom step, where she was sitting. "The hero always falls in love with the girl he rescues."

"Yes, but Emmet's pond is no more than two feet deep," Callie said dryly. "Diana would look a fool pretending to drown in that depth."

"A shallow pond for a shallow owner," Olivia jibed, without turning from the mirror where she was trying to arrange her hood—without any success, if the frown on her face was anything to go by.

"Olivia!" Callie scolded. "If that's a sample of the way you intend to behave this afternoon, then please stay home and spare us all."

"But I couldn't possibly stay home, Callie." Olivia gave her hood a final twitch. "Monsieur d'Armagnac will be there, and I just adore him. I'll wait for you two outside," she added and slipped hastily through the door before Callie could respond.

Callie swallowed uneasily as her stomach lurched protestingly.

"Don't worry, Callie." Diana tried to offer comfort. "Olivia won't do anything she shouldn't. She's just unhappy."

"None of us have cause for unremitting joy, and Olivia's carrying on like a confirmed flirt isn't going to help any!"

"Don't worry," Diana repeated. "I'll talk to her." She buttoned her pelisse hurriedly, tied on her hood, and followed Olivia through the front door.

"Poor Livy." Rosalind sighed. "It must be terrible to love someone who doesn't love you."

"Hmmm," Callie murmured, making a show of looking for her mittens and suppressing the momentary image of Rutledge that flashed through her mind. Rosalind was right. Giving your love where it wasn't reciprocated created a special kind of hell, and one from which, Callie had the frightful premonition, she wouldn't escape. For, Callie admitted with a flash of insight, a great deal of her lingering bitterness over Frederick's defection had been injured pride that he could have treated her with such callousness, rather than actual heartbreak.

"Callie, why are you frowning so?" Rosalind's worried voice penetrated her thoughts.

"Oh, I was just wishing that you were coming with us, dear." Callie kissed her sister's cheek.

"Don't be. I wouldn't like it." Rosalind gave her a hug. "The cold makes my arm hurt, and wouldn't I look a fool trying to skate with my limp. So don't feel sorry for me. I'll be spending the afternoon reading to Papa, drinking hot chocolate, and pitying you all freezing over on Emmet's pond."

"See that you do." Callie laughed and gave Rosalind another hug as she heard the pony trap drive up. "I'd best hurry. It's too cold to keep the poor beast standing."

"Good luck," Rosalind called after her.

And she would need it too, Callie thought as she climbed into the pony trap, seated herself beside her silent sisters, and urged the reluctant pony into a trot.

Callie and her sisters were the last ones to arrive. The other members of the skating party were already assembled. Some of them were sitting on the two long benches which had been placed in front of the roaring bonfire about six feet from the edge of the small pond, and some were already skating on the thick, silvery-gray ice. Callie waited until her sisters had scrambled out of the trap and then handed the pony over to one of Emmet's grooms. She looked around nervously for her quarry. To her dismay, she located him quickly out on the ice with Mrs. Parr.

"Callie!" Ada bustled up, her plump figure well upholstered in red wool. "I was hoping you'd get here earlier. She's already got her claws into him." Ada nodded toward Mrs. Parr, who was being helped across the ice by a laughing Rutledge.

"I think I miscalculated, Ada," Callie mourned, watching

Mrs. Parr move cautiously away from the protection of Rutledge's grasp. "All I thought about was that Diana would show to advantage on the ice. I didn't consider that Mrs. Parr's obvious helplessness would appeal to the earl."

"I think that Mrs. Parr herself appeals to him, and never mind the helplessness!" Ada replied tartly. "It's so frustrating that such an intelligent man could be so blind when it comes to women!"

"It's because he isn't blind that she appeals. I take it Mr. Parr didn't come?" Callie took another quick glance around.

"No," Ada replied, dashing Callie's hopes. "He drank himself into his usual stupor and was snoring in the study when we left."

"Damn!"

"Calpurnia!" Ada sounded scandalized. "You mustn't say such things."

"Damn! Damn! Damn!" Callie repeated, gaining considerable satisfaction from even such a small tilt at society's conventions.

"Let's skate," Ada urged to distract her.

"All right, but first I must find Diana." Callie looked out on the pond, but only Mrs. Parr and the earl were visible.

"They're over there." Ada pointed to the roaring bonfire. Diana and Olivia were seated on one of the plain wooden benches. James Kershaw and Monsieur d'Armagnac were solicitiously helping them to put on their skates.

"The ubiquitous ward." Callie grimaced. "I'd wager that, if we ever do manage to bring this marriage off, Rutledge'll probably send his ward along on the honeymoon."

"You know, Callie—" Ada began, only to be interrupted by Emmet Hadley.

"Afternoon, Callie," he greeted her. "Going to skate?"

"Of course." Callie held up well-worn skates. "I was just going over to put them on. Come with me?"

"Oh, by all means. Let's break up love's young dream," he replied acidly.

Callie glanced at Ada, who raised her eyebrows and shrugged as if disclaiming all responsibility for Emmet's ill-humor.

"Oh, there's Gervais waving for me," Ada said. "I must go. I promised him I'd help him keep his balance."

"Losing three stone would help more," Emmet sniped after Ada left.

"Listen, Emmet Hadley, if you're planning on acting like this all afternoon, then you can jolly well skate by yourself. I don't need you to spread gloom all over my day."

"You're right." Emmet sighed. "I'm behaving abominably, and I'm the host, too. Come on, you can help me tie my skate strings. I haven't mastered tying things with only one hand yet."

"My pleasure, sir." Callie took his arm and started toward the benches. "In return, you can help me figure out a way to get rid of Mrs. Parr."

"Do you want to kill her?" an excited voice whispered from right behind them.

"Abner!" Callie stopped and stared down at the small boy. "You mustn't sneak up on people."

"Why not?" Abner wriggled in between them. "I find out lots of things that way."

"Yes, but they're usually things you aren't supposed to know."

"If you didn't say things you didn't want anyone to hear, you wouldn't have to worry about anyone listening." Abner's air of righteousness made Callie long to smack him.

"Yes, Callie?" Emmet drawled, his blue eyes alight with laughter. "Explain to the child."

"Oh hush, Emmet!" Callie snapped and then peered closer to Abner as the front of his jacket moved.

"Abner, what have you got?" She paused as the truth struck her. "That execrable feline!"

"Execrable feline?" Emmet looked confused.

"She just means George." Abner looked around to make sure his mother wasn't watching, and then undid the top two buttons of his jacket. Immediately, a small fury head popped out and looked around with interest.

"Execrable feline," Emmet agreed. "May I ask why you've got it inside your clothes?"

"Because Mama would never have let me bring him otherwise." Abner looked pityingly at Emmet for being thick-headed.

"It's a mangy barn cat with a penchant for disaster," Callie related.

"That's not fair!" Abner hotly defended his pet. "Things happen to him only when you're around."

"Your rebuttal." Emmet turned to Callie.

"Abner, dear," his mother called from the middle of the pond where she was trying to hold up a very unsteady Gervais. "Come and help your Papa."

Abner hastily shoved George's head back into his jacket and buttoned himself up.

"Hang the ends of your scarf down the front of your jacket, Abner. It will help hide the bulge. Here." Callie reached down and adjusted it for him. "There, off you go."

"Thanks, Aunt Callie."

"You can thank me by keeping that apprentice nemesis away from me."

"Abner!" Ada's shout saved Callie the necessity of explaining about "nemesis" as Abner hurried over to his mother.

Callie put on her skates and then helped Emmet to tie his, trying not to draw attention to his inability to do it himself.

"Thank you, Callie." Emmet rose to his feet and began to traverse the five feet to the pond. "It's not being able to do the little things like tying a woman's skates that drives home my own lack of masculinity."

"What a bag of moonshine!" Callie snorted. "Masculinity doesn't depend on trifling things like tying skates, and if you weren't so sunk in self-pity, you'd see it."

"Nonetheless," Emmet continued with dogged determination, "I couldn't do all the things a woman has a right to expect from a husband."

"You could love her, give her children, and support her in luxury, never mind just the necessities. How many women do you think are fortunate enough to have all that?" Callie demanded. "And all you can do is blather about your lack of an arm. I'm beginning to think it would have been a whole lot better if they'd just killed you, since you seem intent on carrying on as if you're dead anyway. Good heavens, man, you aren't even unique! Plenty of men have lost an arm or a leg in this war, and very few of them had the material resources to fall back on that you have!" With a final glare at the dumbfounded Emmet, Callie started skating toward the center of the pond. She resisted the impulse to look back at Emmet, despite the fact that she felt awful about what she'd said. But someone had to say it. Emmet was sinking deeper and deeper into despair, and soon it would be impossible to reach him at all.

"You skate very well, Aunt Callie." Rutledge's voice from right behind her startled Callie out of her absorption, and she jerked around, losing her balance in the process and collapsing in a heap on the hard ice.

"Thank you," Callie said ironically, trying not to show her pleasure that he'd sought her out. She glanced around for Mrs. Parr, locating her almost at once with the Frenchman and James Kershaw, each holding one of her arms while she attempted to skate. Olivia and Diana were standing on the sidelines, glaring at the sight.

"Poor Aunt Callie." Rutledge reached down, pulled her to her feet, and held her steady against his hard body while he brushed the snow off her skirt. His firm hands swept over her hips, and Callie gulped at the tightening sensation in her stomach. The memory of his kisses was still vivid in her mind, and she licked suddenly dry lips while she reminded herself that he belonged to Diana.

"Thank you, my lord." Callie retreated slightly, favoring the leg she'd landed on. "I'm not usually so clumsy."

"Did you hurt your leg?" Rutledge demanded.

"Limb, not leg!" Callie corrected impatiently. "Ladies don't have legs."

"What strange company you must keep." Rutledge grinned at her. "All the ladies I've ever known have had legs, and very nice ones, too."

"Theron, dear." Mrs. Parr's petulant tones carried clearly over the ice. "I need your help. They aren't as experienced as you are."

"No doubt!" Callie gasped as she realized she'd spoken aloud.

"Now, now, Aunt Callie," Rutledge warned her. "You should have a little more patience for dear Dorcas. She doesn't have your sense of adventure."

"Really?" Callie said dryly.

"Theron!" Mrs. Parr's voice sharpened.

"I won't keep you, my lord." Callie moved back slightly, too proud to compete for his attention. Refusing to look at him in spite of his maddening chuckle, Callie quickly skated away toward the Vardens.

"Why don't you let me help?" she offered, stopping a perspiring Gervais, who was being held up by a flustered looking Ada.

"Would you, Callie?" Ada greeted her with open relief. "Abner was too short. It threw poor Gervais off balance."

"Can't seem to get the knack." Gervais grabbed hold of Callie's shoulder like a drowning man thrown a lifeline. "Can't say as I want to, neither," he added.

"Don't be a goose, Gervais," Ada scolded him. "We've got to do something to entertain our guests."

"I suppose." Gervais took a hasty slide forward, wobbled frantically, and managed to remain upright, much to Callie's surprise. "But I wish they were all as easy as Mr. Parr. Put a bottle of brandy in front of him in the morning, and you don't need to worry about him till bedtime."

"Or put the earl in front of his wife, and you don't have to worry about *her* until the next morning!" Ada snapped.

"Now, dear." Gervais looked puzzled. "It isn't like you to be unkind. I don't understand why you don't like the poor little thing."

"Poor little thing!" Ada gasped. "If she's a poor little thing, I'm the queen!"

"Why, look how brave she is." Gervais pointed to Mrs. Parr, who was attempting to skate away from the earl. Waving her hands madly, she wobbled toward Abner, shrieking prettily the whole distance.

"The poor little thing has good lungs," Callie observed.

"Good everything," Gervais agreed unwisely and then lost his balance and fell when Ada jabbed him in the ribs.

Callie looked down at the sprawled Gervais and swallowed her laughter. There was no sense in hurting his feelings, although she was of the opinion that he deserved it. Poor little thing, indeed!

Suddenly a piercing scream rent the air and Callie jerked around, almost falling at the quickness of her movement. She began racing toward Mrs. Parr, who was lying on the ice.

Rutledge reached the woman first and knelt beside her. He ran his hands over her arms and legs, and then, satisfied that she hadn't broken anything, lifted her head off the ice.

"My ankle!" Mrs. Parr moaned. "I've broken my ankle!"

Callie slipped off her mittens and anxiously felt Mrs. Parr's shapely ankle, an action Mrs. Parr, who was sobbing daintily into Rutledge's coat, never noticed. Callie pressed her lips together angrily. It was obvious that Mrs. Parr hadn't broken anything. But she had hit upon a sure way to gain Rutledge's undivided attention.

"It isn't broken," Callie stated bluntly.

Mrs. Parr glared furiously at Callie. "How would you know?" she demanded. "The pain is excruciating! I must see a doctor. Theron, dear." Mrs. Parr gazed pleadingly at the earl, her huge brown eyes slightly filled with moisture and her perfect ruby lips trembling ever so slightly. She flicked away an imaginary tear and continued, "I feel so faint. I'm too delicate for such active pursuits."

And that was the end of that plan, Callie thought with resignation. Nothing was going the way it was supposed to go. Rutledge should have been disgusted by such a craven attitude, but instead he seemed to be positively relishing Mrs. Parr's helpless demeanor.

"Now, Dorcas," Rutledge's brisk voice braced her, "you've had a shock. I'll take you back to Applewood."

"And tuck her up into bed, I'll wager," Callie mumbled and then flushed scarlet at Rutledge's quick glance, horrified that he might have overheard her.

"James, you and Maurice make a chair with your hands

and carry Mrs. Parr to the carriage. I'll drive her back."

"Oh, Theron." Mrs. Parr moaned theatrically.

"Do as you're told, my dear." Rutledge helped her into the men's arms and then turned to Callie.

"Miss Sutcliff."

"My lord," Callie responded.

"I'll be back for dinner," he said. "I'll tuck Mrs. Parr up into bed, but I don't intend to stay and share it with her."

Callie's strangled gasp went unnoticed as Rutledge followed Kershaw and d'Armagnac and the still-sobbing Mrs. Parr off the ice.

What else could go wrong? Callie wondered with a despairing sigh. Not only had Mrs. Parr gotten the earl to herself, but Callie had most certainly alienated him with her ill-advised remark. She squirmed in embarrassment. Whatever could have possessed her to have said it? Jealousy, she answered honestly. Jealousy at the attention Rutledge was showing Mrs. Parr. Oh God, what a hopeless tangle, she moaned silently, biting back the tears that threatened. No matter what, she couldn't allow them to fall. She had more pride than that. She'd hold her head up and see this evening through as if she hadn't a care in the world.

- 10 -

CALLIE PAUSED IN the doorway of the breakfast room, and an overwhelming feeling of helplessness washed over her as she studied her three younger sisters grouped around the table. Somehow she had to bring their plan to fruition for their sakes, to say nothing of her poor father's.

"Callie." Rosalind looked up and caught sight of her. "Where have you been? You look all peaked."

"It's the fashion," she quipped, passing off her paleness which was the result of an almost sleepless night. "I've been sitting with Papa. He's feeling low because he can't make his left hand do what he wants it to do."

"Poor dear. I'll sit with him later and help him with his notes," Diana offered.

"Thank you." Callie sank down into the empty chair at the foot of the table. "Would you pour me some of that tea, Livy?"

"Cream, sugar?" Olivia waited for an answer, and, at the shake of Callie's head, handed her a cup of tea.

"Don't you want anything to eat?" Rosalind looked wor-

141

ried. "You look thinner than you were."

"I've more important things on my mind than food."

"More important than cream buns?" Olivia teased. "That sounds like heresy to me."

"What's wrong, Callie?" Diana asked.

"Everything!" Callie put her elbows on the table and supported her chin with her hands. "Absolutely everything! The only thing that's gone right is that we haven't seen the vicar since Ada's ball." She paused and turned expectantly toward the door.

"What are you looking for?" Rosalind followed her gaze.

"With my luck recently, that should have been Price's cue to announce the wretched man."

"Really, Callie, you're becoming positively gloomy!" Olivia scolded her.

"And why not?" Callie moaned. "We've tried everything and nothing has worked. We dressed Diana in a gorgeous dress and let the earl see her. We tried to show him what a marvelous hostess she'd make. We attempted to convince him that she shared his interest in sports. We even reminded him of his obligations to the succession." Callie threw a rueful look at the beaming Rosalind. "And what have we to show for it? Nothing! Oh, I admit," Callie rushed on as Diana started to say something, "the earl is polite, charming, and as slippery as an eel. I don't see how we're ever going to bring him up to scratch without putting a gun to his head!"

"Callie?" Diana nervously crushed her napkin into a tight ball and looked fearfully at her sister. "Callie, if it's all the same to you, I don't want him to come up to scratch." She gulped and hurried on, her voice rising with the strength of her feelings. "I tried and tried to like him, but I can't. He frightens me. I can't marry him, Callie! I just can't!"

"It's all right, Diana." Callie's tired voice tried to comfort her. "No one wants you to marry someone you don't like. It was a stupid idea anyway." She sighed. "I should have realized that, if trapping an earl was all that easy, someone would have done it already."

"You don't mind?" Diana released the mangled napkin

and stared at Callie, tears of relief standing in her eyes.

"Of course I don't mind," Callie lied. "We'll think of something else."

"Well." Diana glanced shyly at her sister. "If you really don't mind, I'd like to marry James."

"James Kershaw!" Callie stared at the radiant Diana in stupefaction. "But how, I mean..."

"He's so gentle and kind and sweet and comforting."

"And willing?" Callie demanded.

"Oh, yes, and he can't bear to wait until he's five-and-twenty," Diana replied.

"Why five-and-twenty?" Called asked.

"Because he's the earl's ward," Olivia said, taking up the tale, "and according to James, the earl's already warned him that he'd not sanction an early marriage."

"Did you know about this, Livy?" Callie asked.

"Yes, I did, and if you hadn't been so busy with your own plans, you'd have noticed it, too."

"Oh, Callie, please don't be hurt," Diana pleaded. "I did so want to marry the earl to please you, but when James said he loved me..." Her voice trailed off in remembered bliss.

"I seem to have made a complete botch of things." Callie sighed.

"Don't mind me." Olivia grimaced. "I think my disappointed hopes have embittered me."

"If that means you're being ghastly, you're right!" Rosalind glared at Olivia.

"Not now, girls." Callie absently chopped off the incipient quarrel.

Diana and James. Callie weighed the idea, finding that the more she considered it, the more the marriage had to recommend it. Not only would it solve the problems of her father's peace of mind and her sisters' futures, but on the surface the match would appear to offer Diana a very real chance of happiness. And while Callie could see a host of problems arising if Rutledge persisted in his opposition, none of them seemed insurmountable. Certainly none of them would be as difficult as trying to bring Rutledge up to scratch had been. What she needed now was more information.

"Diana, you're sure that James Kershaw loves you and wants to marry you?"

"Oh, yes." Diana's eyes glowed. "He says he'll do whatever is necessary to make me his."

"Couldn't he just talk to the earl?" Callie suggested.

"No!" Diana blanched at the thought. "I told you, Callie, the earl's already told James that he wouldn't consent to his marriage while he was his ward. And James is only two-and-twenty so that's three whole years."

"I can't say as I blame James," Olivia admitted. "The earl is the most formidable man I've ever met. I wouldn't want to be the one to break the news to him."

"Oh, fiddle!" Callie snapped. "Rutledge isn't anywhere near the ogre you two make him out to be."

"I'll admit you don't seem to have any trouble talking to him," Olivia agreed, "nor that Mrs. Parr, but everyone else keeps a respectful distance."

"We don't talk to him—I quarrel and Mrs. Parr purrs, but that's beside the point. Someone has to tell him."

"No!" Diana jumped up in dismay and then burst into tears. "I can't, Callie! You can't! Please, I beg of you. He'll send James to his estate in Northumberland and I'll never see him again."

"Calm down, Diana. I promise I won't tell. For Heaven's sake, sit down."

"Thank you, Callie." Diana sank back down into her seat and proceeded to blow her nose on the much-abused napkin.

"If you aren't going to tell the earl, what are you going to do?" Callie asked. "Wait until James reaches five-and-twenty?"

"No." Diana braced herself and then blurted out, "We're going to elope!"

"Not while I have a breath left in my body." Callie rejected the idea adamantly. "Diana, you can't be so dead to convention as that. You'd never be able to live down the scandal."

"I don't care." Diana's usually placid features were set in mulish lines. "As long as I have James, I don't care about the rest of the world."

"Well, if the scandal doesn't give you pause, consider this. It will take you five days to get to the border, to say nothing of costing at least one hundred pounds. And if the earl is already that much against James's marrying, he'd have plenty of time to overtake you before you could reach Scotland."

"Oh!" Diana's eyes widened with dismay.

"Yes, 'oh!' And I, for one, wouldn't care to have to face Rutledge after he'd been forced to ride hell-for-leather after me," Callie said.

"No, nor would I," Olivia agreed. "There's no telling what he might do."

"Callie, what can we do?" Diana wailed.

"Larissa." Rosalind said.

"Larissa?" Olivia repeated blankly.

"Yes." Rosalind leaned forward, spilling her milk in her eagerness to share her idea. No one noticed. "Remember how in the book, *The Evil Count,* she and her lover foiled the wicked guardian by getting married by special license?"

"Vaguely." Callie searched her memory. "You know, Rosalind, that could be the answer." Callie turned thoughtfully to Diana. "You and your James could go to Brighton and be married by special license. No one would think it too strange, what with Papa having been so sick. They'd think we did it that way to spare him all the fuss and bother of a big wedding."

"Oh, yes." Diana beamed, her normal good humor restored. "And Brighton isn't so far away. If we left early in the morning, we could be there by nightfall."

"But you wouldn't be able to be married until the next day," Callie said.

"I could go along as chaperon," Olivia offered.

"That would help," Callie agreed, "but we're forgetting one thing. If it takes all day to travel and you can't get married till the next day, that gives Rutledge plenty of time to stop you. Even if he didn't miss James until dinner, he could still reach Brighton before morning on that big bay of his."

"Oh, Callie." Diana's lower lip started to tremble.

"Besides," Callie continued, "if Rutledge is against the marriage and controls James' funds, what were you two planning to live on?"

"James says that the earl is a very proud man, and once we were married, he'd allow us enough to live on, especially if I were increasing." Diana blushed at the thought.

"He's probably right," Callie admitted. "Rutledge wouldn't want it to become known that you'd married without his permission. He's not the kind of man to waste time in useless recriminations. Once you're married, he'll accept it—at least outwardly."

"Then what we have to do is to somehow keep him from noticing that James is gone," Olivia stated.

"I don't see how." Callie frowned. "I mean, it's not as though there are so many guests at Ada's that one wouldn't be missed. Besides, Ada says that the earl has been watching James because of that inflammation of the lungs he had."

"That's true." Diana's face fell. "James says that the earl makes him drink hot milk with a raw egg beaten in it every night before he goes to bed."

Rosalind gagged. "That sounds slimy!"

"Knowing men, it's probably got so much brandy in it that they never notice the egg." Callie sniffed. "But at least that proves my point. So, if we can't hide the fact that James has disappeared, we'll have to make it impossible for his guardian to follow."

"How do you propose to do that? Tie him to the bedposts?" Olivia quipped.

"Almost," Callie said thoughtfully, staring off into space. "I'm going to kidnap him."

"Kidnap him!" Olivia gasped and choked on her tea. "But . . . but . . ."

"It's the only way," Callie explained calmly. "We're agreed that James and Diana can't get married unless we can render the earl inactive for a day and a night, and the only way we can do that is to restrain him physically. Am I right?"

"Right," her sisters chorused.

"And how do you plan to kidnap him?" Olivia asked. "In case it's slipped your mind, the man must be well over six feet and he looks as strong as an ox, while you, my impetuous sister, are a bit on the skinny side."

"I'll simply have to drug him," Callie said.

"You won't hurt him?" Rosalind asked anxiously.

"No, I won't hurt him," Callie reassured her. "I'll just give him enough to put him to sleep. When do you want to do it, Diana?"

"Tomorrow. At least, I think so. James is going to come over this afternoon. I'll ask him then."

"Fine. Remember he'll have to see about hiring a closed carriage from the inn because ours is still broken. If he doesn't have enough money, I can let you have some out of housekeeping."

"That would be best," Diana agreed. "James didn't bring much money because he didn't think he'd need it here and he can hardly ask the earl for it."

"No, he can't, can he?" Callie grinned. "Very well, discuss it with him this afternoon."

"How are you going to get him over here to drug him?" Olivia asked.

"I'm not. He'd be sure to suspect something if I asked him to The Meadings. I'll drug him at Ada's."

"Ada's? Won't she object?" Olivia asked.

"I won't ask her until I'm ready to do it. That way she won't have time to worry about it."

"How considerate of you." Olivia giggled.

"It is, isn't it?" Callie chuckled. "Now that we've gotten that out of the way, I think I'll have some breakfast after all. I have a feeling I'm going to need my strength."

By the time the next morning had arrived and the four sisters were gathered in the morning room waiting to put their plan into action, Callie had convinced herself that it was all for the best. Once she'd considered the idea, it was obvious that the shy, introverted James Kershaw would be more suited to her quiet sister, with her exquisite sensibilities, than the earl. Diana wouldn't have understood his brisk manner, and he would have been driven to distraction by her meek demeanor. While Callie still had some deep-seated misgivings about helping the young couple to marry against Rutledge's wishes, she had stifled them successfully. The need to ensure her sisters' future was far more important than pandering to his autocratic pronouncements. After all, she argued with herself, James was over twenty-one, an adult, and surely capable of deciding for himself whether or not he wished to marry.

"That's James!" Diana jumped to her feet at the sound of the front door knocker. "I know it is."

"I imagine you're right." Callie set down the book she'd been pretending to read. "He said he'd be here at eight, and it's almost that now. Have you got everything, Diana?"

"I think so," Diana muttered, and hurried out of the room, Rosalind at her heels, to see if it really were the perspective bridegroom.

"Don't worry, Callie," Olivia said. "I packed her valise for her and I've got the twenty pounds you gave us in here." She held up her blue reticule.

"That should be enough," Callie said, a worried tone in her voice.

"It will be," Olivia assured her. "James has ten pounds of his own, and Mr. Larkin said the post charges would be eight pounds one way—that's sixteen pounds both ways—which leaves fourteen pounds for the minister, the inn, and food. It should be plenty."

"It should be," Callie agreed, "but . . ."

"Don't worry. Everything will be fine. Just see that you manage to do your part."

"I shall. As soon as I drop you off at the inn, I'm going over to Ada's and do the deed."

"I don't envy you your task." Olivia shuddered. "Quite frankly, the thought of the earl as an enemy petrifies me."

"Nonsense," Callie said briskly as she supressed the involuntary quiver Olivia's words caused. "He's just a man."

"If you say so." Clearly, Olivia wasn't convinced.

"Olivia, we're ready." Diana poked her head through the doorway. "That was James."

"You two go get in the cart," Callie said. "I'll be along in a moment. I want to say good-bye to Rosalind."

By the time Callie had delivered her sisters and James to the inn and then made her way to Applewood, she felt almost faint with nerves. Everything depended on her now. She had to manage to delay Rutledge until tomorrow morning, or all their careful planning would go for naught. Feeling like a prisoner on her way to the guillotine, Callie drew up in front of Applewood with a flourish. Ignoring Johnston's startled expression at her paying a visit so early in the morning, she greeted him cheerfully.

"Good morning, Johnston. Would you please have someone stable my pony? I might be a while."

"Yes, Miss Callie."

"Is Ada down yet?"

"Yes, she's in the morning room with Miss Mary, poor mite." He unbent enough to add, "Passed a restless night, she did."

"Thank you, Johnston. I'll announce myself." Callie handed him her pelisse, mittens, and hood and made her way to the morning room.

"Callie, what in the world brings you out at this hour of the morning?" Ada demanded.

"I must talk to you, Ada. Is there anyone else around?"

"No, just me and poor Mary." Ada nodded to the drowsing baby in her arms.

"Poor sweet, she looks all done in."

"You would be, too, if you'd cried all night instead of sleeping. I'll never be so glad of anything as I will when she finally gets this tooth in. But sit down and tell me what you want."

"Good heavens, is that the redoubtable George?" Callie stared down at the mangy-looking cat asleep in one of Ada's striped chairs.

"Yes." Ada sighed. "I finally gave up. Abner kept smuggling it in every time my back was turned, so I asked the groom to get rid of its fleas and give it a bath."

"I don't think it made much difference." Callie looked doubtfully at the scrawny animal.

"Nothing would turn that thing into a house pet, but Abner will love it so. Just give it a push off the chair and sit down."

"There's no need. I can sit here." Callie chose the chair beside it. "I came"—Callie paused, trying to find the best way to put it—"because I need your help, if you will?"

"Of course I'll help you. Just tell me how."

"By helping me to kidnap the earl," Callie baldly blurted out her intentions.

"What!" Ada shrieked and then subsided hastily as the noise roused Mary and she began to whimper. "Say that again," Ada whispered when she had her daughter safely back to sleep.

"I said, I want you to help me kidnap the earl," Callie repeated obligingly.

"That's what I was afraid you'd said." Ada sank back against the sofa. "Am I allowed to ask why, or is it a secret?"

"You'll do it?" Callie demanded.

"Against every instinct for self-preservation I've got, I'll do it, but I'd still like to know why. I thought we'd decided that forcing him to marry Diana wasn't a good idea."

"We did, and it isn't."

Ada looked closer at her friend. "Callie, you aren't going to hold him for ransom, are you?"

"No." Callie scoffed at the idea. "I just need to keep him out of the way until tomorrow morning sometime, so that he can't go to Brighton."

"Oh, come now. I know Brighton hasn't been the same since the Regent took it over, but surely it isn't that bad!"

"You don't understand, Ada. He can't go to Brighton because James Kershaw and Diana are going to be married there tomorrow by special license."

Ada's mouth dropped open and she stared at Callie, for once speechless.

"But when did all this happen? I mean, only yesterday

we were trying to marry her off to the earl."

"Apparently, I've been rather blind about that," Callie admitted. "I thought Kershaw was keeping Diana company on Rutledge's orders, but he was doing it for himself. According to Diana, they're madly in love and want to get married."

"But by special license?" Ada protested. "I can understand why you wouldn't want a big wedding, what with your father still so sick, but wouldn't Diana want the service here with her family around?"

"Normally, yes, but according to Kershaw, the earl refuses to allow him to even consider marriage until he's five-and-twenty, and they don't want to wait three years. That's why I've got to get the earl out of the way until tomorrow. Once he realizes that Kershaw is missing, it would be a simple matter for him to check with the inn and find out that Kershaw hired a carriage to Brighton."

"Yes." Ada patted the restless baby thoughtfully. "I can see your problem, but what I don't see is how you're going to kidnap him."

"It's simple, really." Callie leaned forward in her chair, eager to explain to her friend. "I'll take some of that laudanum you use for Mary's gums, and put it in his wine. Then, when he falls asleep, I'll take him to that old empty cottage down at the bottom of my apple orchard. The girls and I went down yesterday and got it ready."

"It sounds all right," Ada agreed reluctantly, "but what if something happens while he's unconscious?"

"What could happen?" Callie refused to be deferred. "Besides, I intend to stay with him just in case."

"All night?" Ada's eyes widened.

"Yes. I told Papa that you were giving a party and we three older girls were spending the night with you."

"But your reputation!" Ada protested.

"No one will know. All you have to do, if anyone were to ask, is to say that I felt ill and went to bed early. The earl certainly isn't going to tell anyone that he was held captive overnight by a woman."

"No, I don't suppose he would." Ada considered the

idea. "But, on the other hand, I also can't see him simply forgetting it either. He strikes me as a man who would pay his debts."

"Maybe." Callie ignored the frisson of fear that chased down her spine. "But whatever happens, it'll be worth it. Diana really wants to marry Kershaw, so at least one of my sisters will be happy."

"I do think Diana would be much happier with Kershaw than she would have been with the earl. She and Kershaw are very similar in lots of ways. They should deal famously together. When do you want to do the deed?"

"As soon as possible. I've been building myself up to the kidnapping since yesterday, and I'd like to get it over with."

"I don't blame you. The more I think about it, the more scared I get, but you can't do it at once. Rutledge went out about thirty minutes ago and said not to expect him back until teatime."

"What!" Callie wailed, completely horrified. It had never occurred to her that he might not be there.

"I'm sorry, Callie, but it's true. He often rides out by himself. Remember, I told you that before."

"There's no justice in this world!" she moaned.

"Considering what we're planning, I'd say that's just as well," Ada said dryly. "Besides, you can use the time to prepare the wine."

"Prepare it? I thought I'd just drop some laudanum in his glass and then fill it up with wine."

"Too risky. He might see you do it. We'd do better to mix the laudanum with a whole bottle of wine. Then he won't suspect anything."

"That's a good idea." Callie viewed Ada with respect. "I'd never have thought of that."

"You don't live with a seven-year-old whose driving ambition is to be a spy. Let me put Mary back in her cradle, and then we can fetch a bottle of Gervais' best Madeira. Perhaps the taste won't be so obvious in it."

By three-thirty the earl still hadn't returned, and Callie felt like a pale shadow of her former self. They had long since prepared the wine and decided on a plan of action once Rutledge did appear, but unfortunately, Callie didn't seem to be able to prepare her mind. It was a turmoil of conflicting thoughts, with the main one being that she couldn't fail now—not when her sister's happiness and the solution to most of her problems was within her grasp.

"He's coming!" Ada rushed into the morning room and cast a hurried glance at the waiting wine bottle. "I saw him pass by the house, and instructed Johnston to tell the earl that I wanted to see him the moment he arrived. Otherwise, he'll go to his room to change his clothes, and then we'll never be able to get him by himself."

Callie swallowed on the rising taste of fear in her mouth and forced herself to respond normally. "Where is everyone else?"

"Gervais and the Frenchman went out to inspect something on the home farm. Mrs. Parr is getting ready for dinner—it takes her four hours. Mr. Parr is cast away, of course, and I haven't the vaguest idea where Tristam is. We shouldn't be interrupted."

"Yes, but..." Callie began only to stop as Johnston announced the earl.

"Ladies." Rutledge bowed and then addressed Ada. "I'm sorry to appear in all my dirt, but Johnston said you wished to see me the minute I came in?"

"That's right. Please sit down." Ada gulped and then blurted out the lie they had rehearsed, "Mr. Kershaw asked Callie to tell you that he would be having dinner with Sir Jason, but would be back by ten."

"Yes?" Rutledge arched a sable eyebrow and studied Callie, who couldn't keep her fingers from fidgeting nervously. "It was kind of you to come all this way just to pass on that young scamp's message."

"Oh, but I was coming anyway," Callie rushed to assure him. "I had to see Ada about... about..." For a moment, her mind was horrifyingly blank, and then thankfully something occurred to her. "A parish matter."

"Don't tell me Marston's here!" Rutledge demanded.

"No, it's a feminine parish matter," Callie improvised

wildly. "Nothing that would interest you, my lord."

"You underestimate me, Miss Sutcliff." The earl's lips twitched. "I am interested in all things feminine."

Deeming it time to rescue her friend, Ada entered the conversation. "Do have some wine, my lord." She picked up the bottle to pour it.

"I'd rather have some of that hot tea." He nodded toward the steaming pot from which Callie had been drinking shortly before he arrived.

"It's empty."

"It's cold."

Both Callie and Ada spoke simultaneously.

"It would have been cold if we hadn't emptied it first," Callie amended with a quick frown at Ada.

"In that case, I'll have the wine, but you two must join me. I have an inherent dislike of drinking alone."

"Of course," Callie said brightly, "but just a little. I'm afraid I have no head for wine."

"What *do* you have a head for, Aunt Callie?" Rutledge murmured, low enough so that Ada, who was pouring the drinks, couldn't hear.

"My l-lord?" Callie gazed anxiously at him, too unnerved to parry wits with him.

"Here you are, my lord." Ada handed the earl a full goblet and Callie one half-full.

"Aren't you having any, Mrs. Varden?" Rutledge inquired.

"I'd love some," Ada affected a sigh, "but I nurse the baby, you know, and wine is bad for her."

Callie gave Ada a look of pure admiration at having thought of such an unassailable excuse, and then raised the goblet to her lips, pretending to sip some.

"Mama!" Abner burst into the room rudely awakening George. "Papa said—"

"Abner!" Ada jumped up and rushed to the door with a nervous glance at he earl. Callie set her glass down on the buhl table in front of the sofa and hurried after Ada. There was no telling what Abner had found out, or what he was liable to say. They mustn't alarm Rutledge, now that they actually had the drugged wine in his hand.

"It's nothing, Callie," Ada whispered.

"Nothing!" Abner sounded outraged.

"Nothing that need concern us now, Abner. I'll be up to the nursery later. You go on up now."

"But Mama!"

"Go now, Abner, and I'll buy you a whole sack of bull's-eyes the next time we're in the village." Ada said, casting her principles to the wind and frankly bribing him.

"A whole sack?" Abner eyed her suspiciously.

"A whole sack," Ada repeated, "but only if you go now."

"All right." Abner was obviously won over. "I'll go. 'Bye, Aunt Callie."

"Thank goodness." Callie sighed and turned back into the room.

"George!" she shrieked as she caught sight of the cat standing on the buhl table calmly lapping up her wine as fast as he could.

"My God, he drank the wine!" Ada stared at the mangy creature, half in fear and half in hope of the possible consequences.

"We both did." Rutledge held up his empty glass. "You were correct, Mrs. Varden. The wine was much more refreshing than the tea. Now, if you'll excuse me." He set the empty goblet down on the table beside George's and stood up. "I'll change my clothes."

"No!" Callie blurted out.

"No?" Rutledge smiled blandly at her. "You don't approve?"

"It's not that." Callie flushed at the question. "I meant please don't go yet. I've been wanting to ask you about Northumberland ever since you've arrived, and this seems like a good time."

"As you wish." Rutledge reseated himself, to her infinite relief. "What would you like to know?"

"Anything—I mean everything," Callie said brightly.

"Rather a broad directive," Rutledge observed, but obligingly leaned back in his seat and began a rambling monologue about the Northumberland countryside and people, of which Callie heard only every fifth word. Finally, after what seemed like ages, Rutledge began to slur and he dropped his head back against the sofa, yawning hugely.

"So sorry," he muttered before his head lolled back and his body slumped sideways.

- *11* -

"My lord?" Callie whispered, then cleared her throat and in a louder voice repeated, "My lord?"

Rutledge neither moved nor answered, but remained sprawled limply on the sofa.

"I think it worked!" Ada gazed at him in fascinated horror. "He's asleep."

"Yes." Callie's breath came out in a long whistling sigh. "We did it. Now let's get him to the carriage. I want to get to the cottage before dark." She stood up and walked over to the earl's inert body.

"How?" Ada asked.

"How what?" Callie turned and looked blankly at her co-conspirator.

"How are you planning to get him out to the carriage?"

Callie paused to consider the problem. "I never thought about it, Ada. I was so worried about getting him to actually drink the wine that I never planned beyond that point."

"Well, start planning, because Gervais and the French-man could arrive at any time."

157

"We should be able to move him. After all, there's two of us and only one of him. I'll pull him off the sofa, and you grab his other arm and help me carry him out."

Ignoring Ada's protests, Callie grabbed one of Rutledge's limp arms and pulled, but she succeeded only in shifting his body slightly to the left.

"Pull harder!" Ada urged.

"I can't. I'm afraid I might hurt him." Leaning over, Callie slipped an arm around his waist and yanked upward, only to lose her balance and sprawl on top of him when he didn't budge. Hastily she scrambled up, sniffling tearfully. "Oh, Ada, what are we going to do? We can't move him and we can't leave him here."

"We *certainly* can't leave him here," Ada agreed. "Gervais is a very understanding husband, but somehow I don't think he'd understand this."

Callie squared her shoulders. "Well, if we can't move him, then we'll have to find someone who can."

"Such as?"

"We'll ask a couple of footmen," Callie improvised. "We can say that he just drank too much."

"When they saw him perfectly sober not thirty minutes before?" Ada objected. "Besides, the usual thing to do would be to take him to his room. God knows they have enough practice. They carry Mr. Parr up every night."

"I don't care what they think as long as they do as they're told. It's a little late to change our minds."

"True," Ada agreed, looking down at the earl's still form. "Much too late. Very well then. I'll get two of the footmen to carry him out. They'll have to go with you, too, because you'll never be able to get him into the cottage by yourself."

Callie considered the point. "Yes, and, if you don't mind, I think I'd best borrow your closed carriage. The fewer people who see him the better."

"Amen to that," Ada agreed wholeheartedly. "Do you think we ought to put him in his coat? The snow's melting, but it's still quite cold out there."

"No, it would be too hard to get him into it. I'll cover

him up with one of the carriage rugs. He'll be warm enough.
The cottage isn't very far."

"Shall I send someone after you tomorrow morning?"

"No," Callie said, "we'll walk up to the house, and he
can borrow one of the horses."

"All right, then wait here while I order the carriage and
find the two footmen who usually carry up Mr. Parr," Ada
said and hurried out the door, closing it behind her.

Callie sank down to wait beside the immobile earl, spending her time studying his face. He was so still that she felt
a momentary flash of panic that they might have inadver-
tently harmed him. She picked up one limp wrist and felt
for a pulse, but all she could hear was her own blood pounding in her ears. Leaning over him, she opened his coat and
unfastened two buttons in the middle of his shirt. She pushed
a small cold hand inside to try and find a heartbeat. To her
infinite relief, she immediately felt a heavy, steady beat.

She let out her breath on a long sigh, removed her hand,
and then rebuttoned his shirt.

"Sam and Jack will help us," Ada said, bursting into the
room. "They'll take him to the cottage."

"That's nice," Callie murmured inanely and moved out
of the way as the two husky footmen lifted the earl.

"Take him right out to the carriage," Ada instructed.
"We'll be there in a moment."

"That's everything then," Callie said. "Thank you for
helping me, Ada."

"Thank me after we find out how all this turns out."

"Good-bye, Ada."

"Good luck, Callie. You're going to need it. Oh, wait
a minute." Ada's voice halted Callie as she reached the
door. "Here." She scooped up the flaccid George. "Please
take him with you, Callie. If Abner comes back and finds
out what we've done to his wretched cat, he'll never forgive
us."

"My pleasure." Callie accepted the animal. "He can keep
Rutledge company."

By the time the carriage was actually moving, Callie had

recovered most of her spirits. The worst was over. All she had to do now was to keep him there until tomorrow morning, by which time Diana and her James would be safely riveted.

She felt the carriage slow to a halt and stuck her head out the window to see why they'd stopped. Emmet Hadley was sitting astride a horse by the side of the road.

"Afternoon, Callie," he greeted her. "I thought you were Ada. What are you doing in her carriage?" Emmet urged his horse forward alongside the carriage.

"Oh," Callie gulped, "I'm going for a ride. I'm in a bit of a hurry, Emmet, so if you'd—"

"What are you plotting, Callie?" Emmet rode closer and peered in the window.

"Plotting?" Callie's voice came out in a squeak. "Why should you—"

"Cut line, girl," Emmet interrupted her ruthlessly, "and tell me what's under that blanket." He pointed to the huge lump that Rutledge made under the gray woolen blanket on the opposite seat.

"Oh, that." Callie tried to sound nonchalant.

"I'm waiting, Callie, and I want an answer. I've known you all my life and I'd be willing to bet my last shilling that you're up to no good."

Callie briefly debated making a run for it and then gave up the idea. Emmet could easily overtake the carriage. Her only hope was to tell him the truth and then bind him to secrecy.

"Actually, Emmet, it's the earl."

"It's what!"

"That's right, Mr. Hadley." Sam from the box decided to help her. "It be the Earl of Rutledge."

"What the devil are you doing with Rutledge under a blanket!"

"Keeping him warm," Callie answered. "It's cold out here."

Emmet closed his eyes briefly as if praying for strength and tried again. "Why is he lying there?"

"Because we drugged him."

"We?"

"Ada and I."

"I should have known Ada would be mixed up in this somehow."

"She didn't want to be," Callie's sense of fairness made her admit, "but she helped me because she's my friend."

"If that's a hint for me to do the same, you can forget it. Listen to me, Callie, this isn't some hey-go-mad lark you're involved in. This is serious. Rutledge is a peer— and not just any peer, but a very wealthy, influential one. What do you suppose he's going to do when he wakes up?"

Callie pressed her lips together. "He won't wake up until morning."

"God give me strength!" Emmet clenched his teeth in exasperation. "And what then?"

"It won't matter by then. They'll be safely married."

"Who?" Emmet shot the question at her.

"Diana and James Kershaw."

"I think you'd best explain in a little more detail." Emmet leaned back in his saddle. "What does James and Diana's marriage have to do with your kidnapping the earl?"

"It's very simple, really," Callie explained for what felt like the hundredth time. "The earl won't allow Kershaw to marry until he's five-and-twenty and they don't want to wait three years. So they went to Brighton to be married by special license. Olivia went along as chaperon."

"You surprise me," Emmet said dryly. "With your sense of the dramatic, I would have expected a bolt for the border and a marriage over the anvil in Gretna Green."

"Don't be vulgar, Emmet." Callie sniffed. "Elopements aren't at all the thing, to say nothing of the expense. Besides which, I doubt if I could have managed to have kept Rutledge prisoner for as long as it would have taken them to reach Scotland."

"I wouldn't have thought anything would have fazed you." He paused as what she'd said registered. "Callie, if they didn't have enough money to go to Scotland, how are they planning on paying for the special license?"

"Oh, they took thirty pounds to cover expenses."

"My dear bird-witted friend, a special license costs a hundred pounds."

"A hundred pounds?" Callie whispered.

"And can be obtained only from a bishop."

"A bishop?" Callie gulped back the tears that threatened. "I doubt that Kershaw knows a bishop, even if he had a hundred pounds, which he doesn't. Oh, Emmet," Callie wailed, "what am I going to do? Can't you help?"

But Emmet seemed dumb to her plea as he sat there staring off into the distance. "I'll help you, Callie, but only if you promise to truthfully answer a question first."

"Yes, of course." Callie fell all over herself to agree. "Anything!"

"How serious is Olivia about that damned Frenchman?"

"What?" Callie asked blankly.

"You heard me. If you want my help, then answer the question."

Callie briefly weighed the enormity of the predicament she was in against Olivia's pride and then blurted out, "She isn't. She didn't want you to know how much your fickleheartedness hurt, so she flirted with d'Armagnac."

"Thanks, Callie." Emmet grinned boyishly at her and turned his horse's head.

"Wait, Emmet!" Callie stuck her head further out the window. "Where are you going?"

"Back home to get some money and then to Brighton. I can be there before morning. Don't worry. Unlike the young lovers, I *do* know a bishop, and I've plenty of money."

"Thank you, Emmet." Callie beamed at him.

"I just hope you gave him enough laudanum. I don't relish the thought of a mill with him."

"I did," Callie yelled after him as his horse broke into a gallop. "Go ahead, Sam," she called up to the box and then settled back as the carriage started up again. She carefully studied the blanket-clad lump that was the earl, but as far as she could see in the darkening light, he hadn't moved a muscle.

"Here we be, Miss Callie," Sam called down as the carriage gave a final lurch before coming to a rest in the rut-filled pathway that served the cottage as a road.

The deserted building was just visible in the gathering darkness, its shabby disrepair giving it a lonely, forlorn look.

Jack opened the carriage door and helped Callie out before he stuck his head inside to take an apprehensive look at the earl. "Still out to it," Jack announced with ill-concealed relief. "Miss Callie, you take that beast and hold open the front door, and me 'n Sam'll carry him in for you."

Callie did as she was told, squeezing back into the tiny room as the two footmen maneuvered Rutledge through the narrow door.

"Put him on the bed, please." Callie nodded to the rough bed in the corner. It wouldn't be up to the earl's usual standards, but at least it was clean. She and her sisters had filled the mattress with fresh straw and brought sheets and blankets from the house yesterday.

The two men lowered the earl gently onto the bed and then stepped back, as if amazed by their daring.

"Would you be needing any more help, Miss Callie?" Jack asked.

"I can manage," Callie assured him, only too aware of their almost pathetic desire to escape, "but I'd appreciate it if you didn't mention this to anyone."

"Not bloody likely!" Sam burst out and then flushed beetred. "Begging your pardon, miss, but we wouldn't tell anyone. It might get back to him, and he's one man I'd rather stay free from."

"Good, then we're agreed," Callie said with a heartiness that didn't ring true. "Thank you again for your help." She shifted the boneless George to the other arm and saw them out the door. For all the world like a hostess seeing off her guests, she thought with an almost uncontrollable urge to burst into hysterical giggles. But one look at Rutledge's sprawled figure drove all thought of laughter from her mind.

She averted her gaze nervously, and took a quick look around the small room that constituted the downstairs of the cottage. A huge, stone fireplace dominated the west wall and Callie eyed it with regret. Much as she'd like the warmth a fire would provide, she was leery of lighting one. Despite the relative isolation of the cottage's position, it was still possible that some late-returning fisherman might see the light reflected through the windows and come to investigate. It was a risk she wasn't prepared to take. Never mind, she comforted herself, there were plenty of blankets to keep her warm until morning. Having convinced herself that everything was exactly as she had left it yesterday, Callie dropped George on the single, wooden chair the cottage boasted and reluctantly approached the bed.

Rutledge was lying in exactly the same position that the footmen had left him. Taking a deep breath, she reached over his body to pick up the woolen blankets lying on the far side of the bed, then almost fainted when he mumbled something and stirred slightly.

Callie jerked back and looked at the earl in dismay, but he seemed to have settled again. She rubbed her aching head and tried to think. They must not have given him a large enough dosage because George, she noted with a quick glance at the chair, was still dead to the world. All the more reason to get him covered up, she told herself, trying to rally her flagging spirits. If he were warm he'd be less likely to wake up. Summoning all her determination, she bent over him again and grabbed the blanket. To her horror, her actions roused him further. He stirred, mumbled something that sounded like "darling," and, grabbing her around the waist, pulled her down on top of him.

Callie landed heavily on Rutledge's chest and immediately tried to wiggle off. She thought she'd succeeded as she landed beside him, but he rolled over, pinning her to the mattress with his body. Now what? She flogged her exhausted mind, but it registered nothing but apathetic despair. She lay beneath him, waiting with dull resignation for him to wake up, but to her unbounded relief he didn't. He seemed to have slipped back into unconsciousness without realizing that he was half-lying on her.

The heat from his large frame began slowly to penetrate her numbed senses, warming her chilled body. Callie relished the feel of his firm muscles pressing into her softness.

Soon his body heat began to do more than simply warm her. It began to awaken nerve endings, sparking them to a tingling delight. Unconsciously, Callie relaxed, sinking further into the scratchy, straw mattress. She drew a deep breath to try to regain control of her rioting senses, but that only served to force her closer to Rutledge's hard chest. Her breath quickened as he moved restively, and with another muttered endearment began to nuzzle her ear with his warm lips.

She stole a quick glance down at his face, but to all intents and purposes, he was still asleep. Just an instinctive reaction to finding a woman in his bed, Callie quipped to herself, biting back a hysterical urge to giggle. Rutledge's hand came up to fondle her neck gently and she closed her eyes, savoring the burgeoning sensations he was wakening in her.

But she came out of her euphoric haze with a jerk as the hand which had been fondling her ear suddenly slipped inside the neckline of her dress to find and cup her breast. She tried to twist away, and for a moment she thought she'd been successful as his body shifted to accommodate her movements. Somehow though, she found herself more firmly held with his long leg across her thighs and his hand still resting tantalizingly on her breast.

Callie tried to still her erratic breathing as she waited to see what would happen next. For at least five minutes, nothing did, but just as she finally grew accustomed to the heavy weight of his hand and was starting to relax again, his fingers tightened slightly and his thumb began to gently rub over her nipple until it hardened against his palm.

Callie's breath escaped on a sob as a tingling sensation like nothing she'd ever felt before tore through her body. She closed her eyes and stiffened, telling herself that she was scandalized, but the problem was that she didn't for a moment believe it. Despite the fact that she knew Rutledge wasn't even aware of what he was doing, and even if he had been aware of it, it wouldn't mean anything to him, she didn't want him to stop. She loved him, even while she recognized the total futility of it. Rutledge was a wealthy peer, who would undoubtedly marry a beautiful debutante with a handsome dowry. To think of him in terms of love would be insanity. She couldn't hope for even an affair with him. He was a man of high principles, who would never stoop to seducing his hostess's best friend. Besides, Callie thought cynically, she wasn't pretty enough to make it worth his bother. This was all she would ever have to remember. The feel of his heavy body on hers, his sleepy caresses, and a few kisses.

She eyed the earl's sleeping face speculatively and then stirred restively as his hand started its persuasive movements on her breast again. Why shouldn't she kiss him? she asked herself. It couldn't hurt him. He wouldn't even know it and she'd have the experience to remember.

She inched cautiously toward him until her head was level with his, then hesitantly pressed her lips against his firm mouth. Closing her eyes, she savored the feel of his hard lips against hers, unconsciously snuggling closer. She felt his tongue flick across her lower lip and, when she opened her mouth instinctively, Rutledge's lips closed over hers with swift ferocity as he gathered her tightly against his solid chest. For a brief moment, she wondered if she'd awakened him, but her mind stumbled before the toll his experienced lips were taking. She ceased to think about anything and just felt. Excitement broke over her in waves and she pressed closer to him as his tongue penetrated her mouth, slowly, sensually, exploring its softness.

Time and circumstances ceased to have any meaning as she reveled in the sensations his practiced caresses were wakening. She was still lost in a state of euphoric bliss when he shifted his body, and, although his weight still held her pinned to the bed, he now lay on his stomach with his head facing away from her.

Callie whimpered slightly, feeling utterly bereft at the loss of his lips. His arms tightened comfortingly, molding her to his warm side, but he did not turn back.

Callie stared up at the rough ceiling, barely visible in the gloom, and tried to steady her whirling mind. For the first time she was beginning to wonder if perhaps there wasn't some truth in all those heroines who were forever swooning with delight when kissed by the hero. Beside the way she felt right now, a swoon would be a simple matter. She tried to decide what to do about the situation she found herself in, but her exhausted mind was unequal to the task. Slowly, her eyelids closed, and she drifted into a deep, dreamless sleep where the vexing problem of the earl couldn't follow her.

A thudding sound brought Callie to consciousness and she forced open eyelids that felt glued together. She blinked as her eyes focused on the shadowed timbers of the cabin's roof. Confused, Callie glanced around, blushing a brilliant red as her eyes encountered Rutledge's dark shape looming above her.

"What—" she began, but Rutledge clapped a large hand over her mouth.

"Quiet!" he whispered harshly.

The thuds were louder now, and Callie's rapidly awakening mind recognized them as hoofbeats. Hoofbeats from a horse being ridden hard.

Rutledge picked her up and pulled her over against the wall, out of the line of vision of anyone opening the door.

Callie stumbled, mumbling under her breath at the impossibility of seeing clearly in the darkened cabin. The only light was a bright patch of moonlight coming in through the cabin's single window.

"Who lives here?" Rutledge whispered.

"No one," Callie told him. "It's been deserted for well over a year."

The horse pounded up to the door, halted, and someone jumped down. The animal was given a sharp slap that sent him galloping away.

Rutledge pulled Callie behind him and turned to face the door as it burst open.

Tristam Varden was revealed clearly in the moonlight in the instant before he ran in. He didn't run far. He'd covered no more than two feet before there was an earsplitting yowl, a graphic curse, and the sound of a body falling over furniture.

"George!" Callie cried. "I left him asleep on a chair."

"In the doorway, I trust?" Rutledge asked dryly.

"Well, I wasn't expecting company," Callie muttered.

"That's right, this was a private affair. By invitation only, wasn't it?"

Callie winced at his scathing words. It was painfully obvious that Rutledge was not very happy, but in all honesty, she could hardly blame him.

"Do you have any light?" Rutledge demanded as Tristam lay groaning on the floor. There was no further sound from George. Apparently he'd vanquished the enemy and then gone back to sleep. Callie wished Rutledge would do the same, but he didn't seem to be showing any afteraffects from the laudanum as the cat was.

"Yes," she answered his question and took a candle from the mantel where she and her sisters had left some yesterday, struck a flint, and lit it. The taper shed a feeble light over the cabin, revealing Tristam, who was sitting on the floor clutching his arm, and George, who was sound asleep on the chair.

"What are you doing here, Tristam?" Callie demanded, but he didn't answer. He just continued to cradle his arm and moan.

Rutledge knelt down, and, despite Tristam's vocal objections, proceeded to examine him.

"Did he hurt himself?" Callie asked once she'd satisfied herself that George had suffered no harm in the contretemps.

"Not really." Rutledge stood up. "He simply dislocated his shoulder. I can put it back for him easily."

"No!" Tristam jerked away. "Don't touch me! I'm wounded!"

"My good man," Rutledge eyed Tristam with contempt, "I assure you that you're not in any danger. Once your shoulder is put back in place, all you'll have is a slight ache for a day or two."

"I want . . ." Tristam began, only to pale at the sound of pounding hooves in the distance.

"So much for our privacy!" Callie muttered.

"It is becoming rather public," Rutledge agreed. "I realize that, weighed against kidnapping, this may seem like a minor point, Miss Sutcliff, but it is not at all the thing to be caught at night, alone with a man, miles from anywhere. Your reputation would be in shreds."

Her reputation was the least of her worries, Callie thought hopelessly. It appeared that all her careful plans were about to come to naught.

"Tristam has already seen me," Callie pointed out.

"But Tristam isn't going to open his budget, are you, Tristam?" Rutledge's voice was threaded with pure menace.

"No, no," Tristam denied. "It's no bread-and-butter of mine."

"I thought you'd feel that way," Rutledge said silkily. "Up," he ordered Tristam. "You stay here until I come back," he told Callie.

"But you can't go out there!" Callie objected. "You don't know who . . ." She found herself ignored as Rutledge hauled the protesting Tristam up by his coat collar and pushed him through the open door, slamming it shut behind him.

The silence pressed in on Callie, seeming to suffocate her. She bit her lip nervously and tried to think of what to do. She had visions of Rutledge lying wounded, beaten or shot by the unknown men threatening Tristam, and it was all she could do to keep from dashing out after him. He'd said stay, though, she reminded herself. Surely he'd realize the danger and take care. She picked up George and snuggled him close, ignoring his plaintive meows of protest. Just holding another living thing helped, and Callie sat down in the chair while her distraught mind tried to plan.

- *12* -

THE MINUTES STRETCHED BY, each assuming gargantuan proportions, while Callie's imagination ran riot. Visions of Tristam having been chased by thieves and murderers floated through her mind. Finally, after what seemed like hours to Callie's taut nerves, she heard the sound of a man's footsteps overlaid by the clop of a horse's hooves.

"Don't worry, it's me." Rutledge pushed open the door.

"You mean it's I," Callie inanely corrected his English and then burst into tears, totally unable to stem her wild sobbing.

"My poor Aunt Callie." Rutledge plucked her out of the chair and sat down on the bed, cradling her against his chest while murmuring soothing endearments.

"I'm so sorry." She hiccuped. "It's just that . . ."

"That things suddenly got too much for you," Rutledge finished for her. "It has been quite an evening!" He gathered her close with the obvious intention of kissing her, but George took exception to being squeezed, and howled.

"That damn cat!" Rutledge viewed the feline with displeasure. "Did you have to bring him along?"

"I had to do something with him. I mean, you can't just drug someone and leave them by the side of the road, as it were."

"I must admit I hadn't considered the etiquette of the situation. I suppose one does have a responsibility toward one's victims."

"You never were asleep, were you!" Callie jerked herself out of his arms and faced him as the truth suddenly struck her. "You were only shamming!"

"That's right," Rutledge admitted equably. "While you and the good squire's wife were shamelessly bribing young Abner, I poured the wine under the sofa."

"But how did you know?"

"My dear Aunt Callie, you two were the most obvious conspirators I've ever seen. A child would have realized you were up to something."

"Then why pretend to go to sleep?" Callie snapped. "Why not just accuse us?"

"And miss the most entertaining evening of my life?" Rutledge chuckled. "I haven't had so much fun since my Oxford days when we loosened a performing bear in the don's study."

"It isn't funny!" Callie bit out. "When I think of all the trouble we went to and all the worry—" Callie broke off in horror as the full meaning of what he was saying penetrated. If he had never been drugged, then he hadn't been asleep when he'd been kissing her—or, more to the point, when she'd been kissing him.

"You rake!" she screamed at him. "You libertine! Taking advantage of a helpless female."

"Helpless!" Rutledge hooted. "You're about as helpless as the British Navy. I can't think of anyone I'd rather have on my side when I'm in a tight corner."

"Yes, but..." Callie's sense of outrage was only partly mollified by his praise.

"And, if you're waiting for an apology, you'll wait a long time. I thoroughly enjoyed kissing you and caress-ing—"

"You, sir, are no gentleman!" Callie was incensed that he should refer to her wanton behavior in such a cavalier fashion. The least he could do was to pretend that it never happened.

"And what's more," he persisted, "you did, too. But enough of this dalliance. I borrowed a horse from one of Tristam's pursuers so that we could get back to the squire's. Much as I'd like to spend the night here with you, I've several things that need attending to. Come along, Callie." Rutledge pushed her toward the door.

"What time is it?"

"Shortly before ten."

"Is that all!" Callie stopped in surprise. "I thought it was the middle of the night."

"No." He urged her forward again. "We were asleep only for a few hours."

Callie blushed at the intimate sound of what he was saying, and then jumped in fear as a huge horse materialized out of the darkness in front of her.

"It's just us, boy." Rutledge ran a comforting hand down the animal's neck. "Don't be nervous." He turned to Callie. "I don't suppose you'd consent to leave that four-legged disaster behind until morning, would you?" he asked without much real hope in his voice.

"Of course not." Callie cuddled George closer. "He'd be lonesome. And he isn't a disaster. A little accident-prone, perhaps, but definitely not a disaster."

"Ha! Then hold onto him and make sure he doesn't claw the horse. I have no wish to finish off the evening by being thrown into a ditch."

He put his hands around Callie's slim waist and tossed her up into the saddle, then mounted behind her. He gathered up the reins and pulled Callie back against his hard chest before nudging the horse into a trot.

"My lord?" Callie began.

"Do you suppose you could manage to address me as Theron?" he asked.

"Like Mrs. Parr? Thank you, but I prefer to be different."

"My dear Aunt Callie, you are not just different, you are

unique. And there's no reason to be jealous of Mrs. Parr. She served her purpose very well."

"I can imagine." Callie sniffed.

"Possibly, but with your lack of experience, not very accurately.

"My dear sir—" Callie's raised voice caused the horse to shy.

"Never mind, my dear." He patted her shoulder in an avuncular manner. "It's always been my goal to stamp out ignorance. I'll see that you have some firsthand knowledge."

"What purpose?" Callie returned to the subject of Mrs. Parr, deciding to ignore his last taunt.

"To see the countryside. The War Office is drawing up defense plans for the whole coast in the unlikely event that Boney should try to invade England. Since I was coming down to Kent anyway, I agreed to survey the terrain. I didn't want to alarm anyone by letting them know what I was doing, so I needed an unexceptional excuse to be out and about. And what better excuse than to take a beautiful woman driving?"

"She is beautiful," Callie admitted grudgingly.

"Exquisite," Rutledge agreed, "and she has exactly two thoughts in her head—her looks and how they're affecting the men around her. Besides, she has a husband."

"Who is never sober," Callie muttered.

"That's beside the point. I never make love to other men's wives. But enough of Dorcas Parr. I've seen enough of her this last week to last me a lifetime."

"All right." Callie was perfectly willing to consign Mrs. Parr to oblivion. "But would you please tell me what was going on tonight? Who was chasing Tristam and why?"

"Several of the village's young bucks," Rutledge said. "It seems that Tristam has been playing rather deeply."

"And losing," Callie said without doubt.

"And losing," Rutledge confirmed. "He's been staving off his creditors with vague promises, and tonight they decided to take matters into their own hands."

"They weren't going to hurt him, were they?"

"No. According to their leader, all they wanted to do

was to scare him so that he'd get sufficient funds from his brother to pay them. Although I can't say that they weren't pleased that he suffered some discomfort."

"Where is he?"

"They took him back to Applewood."

"Poor Tristam." Callie truly felt sorry for the luckless young man.

"Stupid Tristam, might be more accurate," Rutledge said crisply. "At any rate, he's in for an uncomfortable ride back. He's riding pillion behind one of his creditors, while the other one went for the doctor."

"Poor Ada." Callie sighed. "She's had such a trying day." She turned slightly to glance up at the earl's face. "You won't be angry with her, will you? She didn't want to drug you, but she's my friend, so of course she helped me."

"There's no of course about it," Rutledge said dryly. "This may come as a shock to you, but not all people find friendship a sufficient excuse to engage in criminal activity."

"Criminal activity!" Callie protested. "A simple little matter like drugging you?"

"And kidnapping me," Rutledge added. "You could be transported for less. However, I have another punishment in mind."

"Punishment?" Callie gulped, tightening her hold on George.

"Later, Aunt Callie. We're almost there." Rutledge took a firmer grip on the horse's reins and guided him along the front of the house, stopping by the door.

It was opened the moment they knocked by a very pained-looking Johnston.

"Good evening, Miss Callie, my lord." He ignored the limp feline in her arms. "Won't you—"

"Callie!" Ada's startled voice interrupted him. "What—"

"Good evening, Mrs. Varden," Rutledge greeted her smoothly, taking no notice of her shock. "Do you suppose we might have some tea? For some reason, I seem to have missed my dinner."

"Y-yes," Ada stuttered and then shot an imploring look

at Callie. "Won't you come into the morning room? Johnston, have cook send up some tea and cakes."

Callie trailed along behind Ada and the earl, feeling curiously detached from her surroundings. Instead of refreshing her, her nap had only served to further muddle her already tired mind.

"This is a surprise, my lord," Ada began cautiously.

"Cut line, Ada." Callie dropped George onto the floor and sank down on the sofa, wearily closing her eyes. "He never drank the wine. It was all a hum."

"Never!" Ada's voice was shrill. "But, but . . ."

"Never," Callie repeated. "Poor old George was the only one who got any."

"Well, it seems to have done him nothing but good." Ada eyed the limp beast. "I've never seen him so quiet."

"Only if you don't sit on him," Callie warned with a grin.

"Sit on . . ." Ada began, only to be interrupted by her son.

"Aunt Callie!" Abner burst into the room. "You missed all the excitement."

"What are you doing up, Abner?" Callie asked. "It's gone ten o'clock."

"Uncle Tristam got hisself hurt!"

"Himself," Callie corrected.

"He means it, Callie." Ada forgot the earl for a moment. "Tristam dislocated his shoulder. He says he fell, but we don't believe him. Gervais figures it was probably one of his gambling debts coming home to roost."

"Hmmm?" Callie murmured.

"But Gervais says that this time Tristam's going to the Bahamas to manage the family plantations, even if he has to tie Tristam to the boat himself."

"An excellent idea," Rutledge interjected. "Many's the young man who's straightened himself out in the Colonies. Why don't you tell Tristam that I'll give him a letter of introduction to some friends that I have in Nassau?"

"That's very generous of you, my lord, especially considering . . ." Ada trailed off into an embarrassed silence.

"Just so." Rutledge smiled at her.

"You aren't going to, I mean," Ada fumbled for words. "Gervais wouldn't like it if, I mean..."

"My silence rather depends." Rutledge paused and waited until Johnston had set down the tea tray and departed, taking George with him.

"Silence!" Ada jumped. "That reminds me, Callie. Emmet stopped by tonight on his way to Brighton, and you'll never guess what!"

"Ada," Callie groaned. She'd tried so hard to keep off the subject of why they'd kidnapped the earl in the hope that in all the excitement he wouldn't remember until it was too late to do anything about it.

"But it's good news, Callie," Ada insisted. "Emmet said he was on his way to Brighton to marry Livy by special license."

"Marry Livy!" Callie's mouth dropped open. "But what about his Spanish fiancée?"

"There never was a Spanish lady," Ada said. "Emmet said he made her up because he didn't want Livy to marry him out of pity. Anyway, a blind man could have seen how jealous he was whenever the Frenchman even smiled at her. And speaking of the Frenchman, have you seen him? He wasn't here for dinner, and that isn't like him."

"Yes," Rutledge answered. "I meant to tell you this afternoon, but somehow I got sidetracked. He had to go to Brighton and will return tomorrow."

"Why not?" Callie muttered. "The whole world's in Brighton. Why shouldn't he be there, too? Are you going to try and stop James?" Callie brought the subject out into the open.

"No, why should I?" Rutledge accepted a cup of hot tea from Ada. "I can't say that I'd like to be married to Diana myself. She'd drive me mad within a week, but if he's happy, that's his business."

"But this whole fiasco was caused by your telling him that you'd not let him marry until he was five-and-twenty," Callie exclaimed in confusion.

"Since he was eighteen at the time I said it, and the lady

in question was a thirty-year-old Paphian, I think I was justified."

"Oh, well," Callie sighed, "at least it served to bring Emmet to his senses. But I can't help but feel rather hard done by."

"Surely not, Miss Callie." The Reverend Marston hurried into the room, only to be regarded blankly by all its inhabitants.

"A fitting finale to the evening," Callie muttered.

Ada shot a warning glance at her and turned to the vicar. "Why, Reverend Marston, what brings you visiting?"

"So late," Callie added.

"I heard that the doctor had been called to attend poor young Mr. Varden, and I felt it my sacred duty to lend my moral support to his afflicted relatives in their hour of grief," he explained pompously.

Before Ada could respond, Rutledge interposed. "You're just the man I wanted to see." The earl set down his teacup, rose, and firmly shook Marston's hand—to the good curate's open-mouthed astonishment. "Such devotion to duty, such zeal for carrying out the Lord's work. It leaves me speechless."

"Not noticeably," Callie threw in.

"Yes, m'lord?" Marston shot a reproachful look at Callie.

"You're absolutely wasted here in Thornton Dene." Rutledge cast an apologetic smile at Ada, who gamely rose to the occasion.

"We wouldn't dream of standing in his way," Ada enthused.

"I'm hoping you'll accept a living on my Northumberland estates," Rutledge continued. "Indeed, I shall be bereft if you don't."

"A living?" Marston echoed incredulously.

"Shall we say in the amount of three hundred pounds a year?"

"Oh, yes, m'lord!" Marston grabbed the earl's hand and started pumping it. "I accept with pleasure."

"Good, good." Rutledge rescued his ill-used hand and sat back down. "Don't let us keep you from young Varden.

I'll have my man of business contact you tomorrow."

"Why did you do that?" Callie asked as soon as Marston had left. "I didn't think you liked him."

"I don't, but he's part of an excellent plan I have in mind."

"I hope you're still able to say that after a month of listening to his vile sermons!"

"I have no intention of listening to him," Rutledge said. "My Northumberland estates are quite large. Marston will have a living well away from the castle. I intend to keep him in reserve as a threat."

"A threat?" Ada repeated in confusion.

"To my wife," Rutledge related. "If she doesn't behave herself, I'll have Marston transferred to the castle. The threat of listening to a few sermons like the one we were subjected to last Sunday should be enough to bring the most wayward wife to heel."

"You're getting married?" Ada asked the question that Callie's stricken mind couldn't.

"That's right." Rutledge chose a cake from the tray before he continued. "I intend to take a leaf out of James's book and elope to Brighton."

"Who you gonna marry?" Abner demanded. "Not that gudgeon Mrs. Parr!"

"No, not that gudgeon Mrs. Parr," Rutledge answered. "I plan to marry your Aunt Callie."

Callie gasped and choked, spraying tea all down the front of her crumpled dress.

"Hurrah!" Abner shouted. "I'll come to visit you. I'll even give you George as a wedding present," Abner offered, missing the earl's wince at his generosity. "I think he likes Aunt Callie better'n me anyhow."

"How could you!" Callie slammed down her cup and glared at Rutledge, her lips trembling. That he could tease her about something that meant so much to her was insupportable. "I know we've treated you badly, but that's no reason to, to . . ." She dissolved into tears and ran from the room, intent on escaping.

"Callie!" she heard him shout, but she ignored both the

call and Johnston's startled face as she raced up the stairs toward the sanctuary of a guest room. She ran into the room and, slamming the door behind her, flung herself on the dainty four-poster bed, crying with furious abandon. So great was the depth of her despair that she never heard the door open. Her first intimation that someone else was in the room was when a weight settled on the bed beside her.

"Oh, Ada," she sobbed, "how could he?"

"In self-defense, my dear." Rutledge's strong hands on her quaking shoulders urged her to face him. "I think it would be much safer to keep you beside me rather than to let you run loose."

"That's not funny!" Callie hiccuped.

"It wasn't meant to be." Rutledge eased his long body down beside her and gathered her closely, molding her pliant form to his hard frame. His gentle fingers began to trace sensual patterns on her damp cheek.

Callie closed her eyes momentarily as she savored the feel of being trapped between his muscular body and the firm mattress, but she refused to allow herself to succumb to the erotic motions of his hands. There were too many unanswered questions she needed satisfied.

"My lord—um, Theron," she began, "please tell me why you said what you did."

"Because I meant it, of course, my thick-headed little treasure." Rutledge pushed her tangled hair out of her damp face. "Hasn't it occurred to you yet that I love you?"

"You what!" Callie gasped, her eyes snapping open. "You can't love me. I haven't any money and no looks to speak of."

"I've money enough for both of us, my love, and as for your looks." He paused and studied her face as if committing each separate feature to memory. "You're beautiful, clear through to your loyal little heart."

"Really?" Callie peered wistfully up at him.

"Really." The utter conviction in his voice assured her that he at least believed what he was saying. "The first moment I saw you, hanging there like the fairy on a Christmas tree, I knew you were someone special."

"Then why didn't you tell me before?" Callie snapped, remembering the agony she had gone through.

"Well," Rutledge grinned at her, "I was having too much fun watching you try to marry me off to your bird-witted sister."

"You knew?"

"My dear, I've been stalked by some of the most predatory matchmaking mamas in London," he replied with a great deal of asperity. "Next to them, your efforts were child's play. And I was curious to see what you'd try next. But I will admit that tonight's escapade exceeded my wildest imaginings."

"Mine, too." Callie sighed. "I'm glad I can give up the matchmaking business. It was never this hard in the book."

"Rowena's Reward?" Rutledge queried.

Callie looked at him in surprise. "Where did you hear about *Rowena's Reward?* It was a wonderful book."

"The wife of a friend of mine is fond of it, but no matter. You will marry me, my sweet Callie? I love you to distraction, and to prove it, I'm even willing to accept George as part of the bargain."

"That is rather a daunting thought." Callie chuckled. "Perhaps we can find him a nice barn to inhabit?"

"I doubt it. That cat knows a good thing when he sees one."

There was a moment's pause, and Callie played with one of the pearl buttons on the earl's waistcoat. "Theron?"

"Was there anything else you wanted to know?" Rutledge asked indulgently.

"Not *know...*" Callie's wandering hand reached up and her sensitive fingertips trailed along his hard jaw. The faint scratchiness of his face sent shivers of delight coursing through her arm, and she licked her dry lips with a small pink tongue. *"Do* perhaps..." She arched herself toward him provocatively.

His reaction was instantaneous. He pulled her supple body under his and leaned over her, creating a sensual cage from which Callie had not the slightest desire to escape.

"Yes," his voice was husky, "there is most definitely

something to do." His hand, which had been gently stroking her neck, slipped lower and suddenly pulled down the loose bodice of her dress, exposing a small, firm breast.

Callie inhaled sharply as he tenderly caressed her breast. Desperately wanting the feel of his lips on hers, she strained toward him, but his hands and weight held her captive on the bed and he chuckled.

"Patience, darling, we have all the time in the world." He quickly ran the tip of his tongue around her ear, and then began to place a series of light, tantalizing kisses down her neck, driving Callie frantic. His lips halted momentarily in the valley between her breasts, then leisurely explored the silky softness of the exposed slope. "So soft and smooth and perfect," Rutledge praised as he worked his way to the pink-tipped crest.

Callie gasped in mindless pleasure as his lips closed over the taut nipple and his tongue gently caressed it to trembling rigidity.

"Oh, Theron," Callie cried, throwing her arms around his neck, "I love you so."

"And I you, my darling." His lips closed over hers with savage intensity.

Second Chance at Love

™

All of the above titles are $1.75 per copy

Available at your local bookstore or return this form to:

SECOND CHANCE AT LOVE
Book Mailing Service
P.O. Box 690, Rockville Cntr., NY 11570

Please enclose 75¢ for postage and handling for one book, 25¢ each add'l. book ($1.50 max.). No cash, CODs or stamps. Total amount enclosed: $ _____ in check or money order.

NAME_____

ADDRESS_____

CITY_____STATE/ZIP_____

Allow six weeks for delivery.   **SK-41**

All of the above titles are $1.75 per copy

WHAT READERS SAY ABOUT
SECOND CHANCE AT LOVE BOOKS

"Your books are the greatest!"
—*M. N., Carteret, New Jersey**

"I have been reading romance novels for quite some time, but the SECOND CHANCE AT LOVE books are the most enjoyable."
—*P. R., Vicksburg, Mississippi**

"I enjoy SECOND CHANCE [AT LOVE] more than any books that I have read and I do read a lot."
—*J. R., Gretna, Louisiana**

"For years I've had my subscription in to Harlequin. Currently there is a series called Circle of Love, but you have them all beat."
—*C. B., Chicago, Illinois**

"I really think your books are exceptional . . . I read Harlequin and Silhouette and although I still like them, I'll buy your books over theirs. SECOND CHANCE [AT LOVE] is more interesting and holds your attention and imagination with a better story line . . ."
—*J. W., Flagstaff, Arizona**

"I've read many romances, but yours take the 'cake'!"
—*D. H., Bloomsburg, Pennsylvania**

"Have waited ten years for *good* romance books. Now I have them."
—*M. P., Jacksonville, Florida**

*Names and addresses available upon request